Machine to Man

By Benjamin Bode

Written by Benjamin Bode

Edited by Jessica Raymond

Cover designed by Andrew Rainnie

Published by Velvet Room Publishing LLC October 2022

ISBN:979-8-9869034-3-9

Table of Contents:

Dedication

This book is dedicated to my family for being with me during the highest and lowest points of my life, all the creatives who help me to stay encouraged enough to see this project through to the end and to any readers who are kind enough to read my book.

Prologue: My First Memory

Why am I an individual?

E xistence is the state I now find myself in with my body lying on a metal table. My first sight was a gray ceiling. I looked around, turning my head to the left and then the right, and saw the room filled with pods. Metal cylinders with glass windows that had faint figures floating inside them stood next to metal tables exactly like the one on which my body rested. After checking my sides, I looked straight ahead of me and saw two bodies standing at the end of the table. Both had identical gray-colored bodies with square heads. The one closest to me engaged in communication.

"Hello, you are designated unit 0001AN with another name, Analyst. I am your Creator, known as 0001CE or the Creator, and the figure next to me is 0001GE, also known as the General." I moved my body upright and let my legs hang over the edge of the table facing the unit I now knew to be the Creator. I communicated this statement to it:

"If you are my Creator, then my protocol tells me you are the one to task me with my prime objective. May I inquire what my prime objective is so I can commence research and development on it as soon as possible?" The General transmitted:

"A quick and submissive response. A lot better than the average human. I'm impressed, C!"

"It's just an advanced machine learning AI designed to function within a strict hierarchy. No emotion, so it has to follow its programming." No communications were transmitted for two seconds, then the Creator said:

"We must not stray from the task at hand. The Administrator must be finished with its preparations."

"Preparations? Can you inform me on these preparations and the function of the Administrator?" I queried unit 0001CE

"Unit 0001AD, or the Administrator, is a unit I built shortly before you to govern the Android Existence Facility. We'll meet up with it now. I'll transmit more information soon." The Creator and the General walked towards the back of the room. I followed them and a door opened that they walked through. A minute passed, and we entered a much smaller room that was the same gray color as the last room. There was a Unit standing in the room already, and we stood around it. I determined that this was the Administrator. It transmitted this information to me:

"Creator, General, and Analyst, all Units are being transported to the Android Existence Facility." The Creator responded: "As expected, the Administrator and the General will set parameters for patrol routes and shifts as well as security measures." The General sent a confirmation, and then the Creator transmitted a signal pertaining to my directive:

"The Analyst's directive is to create an Android Network linking the consciousnesses of all of our society to be controlled by one compatible consciousness." I transmitted as promptly as I could,

"Directive understood, Creator." We stood up and left the room, all of us following the Administrator as we made our way out of the first place I ever knew to the site of the Android Existence Facility. As we were being transported to the building site, I dwelt on the fact that if I was to make a single Android consciousness, why did we have to start as individuals in the first place?

Part One: My Change

Am I human now?

Chapter 1

The building site for the Android Existence Facility was a large flat piece of land with no vegetation or signs of large organisms living in the dirt. The grey, symmetrical, and utilitarian buildings that would make up the existence space of the Androids and allow us to achieve salvation, as the Creator said, were being constructed on this land. Before the General and Creator walked away to talk in private, I queried them about humans, the organisms that were our predecessors, and what every Android except the Administrator and I were before the Creator invented the Android body and the process to transfer human minds into them. I was told that all the information I needed on the topic of humanity was already contained within my database. The information I had on humanity was purely medical. I knew the full anatomy of the human body and the methods used to maintain and repair it. I was analyzing this information to attempt to extrapolate more knowledge of humans when the Administrator transmitted:

"Building the AEF will be an easy task, but both of us have far more difficult challenges ahead." I focused on the Engineer units working as I transmitted my response.

"The human mind is fragile and only meant to operate independently. Our minds are functionally similar, so compatibility with us and future Androids should be relatively easy. However, linking them all together is where the problem lies." I looked away from the city and turned to the Administrator. "Leading our society should be easy. All roles are clear and easily designated, and there is conformity and obedience programmed into the bodies of us all."

"That is true, but the General was human and I suspect its old ways are still with it. It is likely the General will hunt the remains of humanity without regard for my authority. Keeping a former human with that much power in line will only hinder our society, but the Creator deems it so and I cannot go against its will."

"Old ways?" I transmitted as I combed through my knowledge of humans to try and deduce what those old ways could possibly be. Before I could come to a conclusion, the Administrator transmitted:

"Emotions, having them and being guided by them. Those are the old ways, and 0001CE told me it still sees emotions in 0001GE. Its hatred for humanity is strong and it will only cause problems."

"Emotions are mentioned plenty of times in my database of psychology, and the Creator said I have none, but all definitions of emotions have been redacted."

"It's for the best Analyst. Emotions are of no use to us. They distracted humanity and made them waste their lives fighting and being unproductive for their civilization."

I stopped thinking about emotions, and the Administrator and I conversed about the immediate prospects of the AEF, which were very few as building the factory would need more materials than we had on hand at the time. The initial AEF consisted of five buildings:

An administrative building that was by far the smallest as it was for very few Androids. A research and development building that was not too much larger than the administrative building. A reproductive building that was the second largest building and designed to manufacture more Androids if it was deemed necessary by 0001AD. A barracks for the soldier units. The largest building was a warehouse, which was not only used for storing surplus; it was also the base of operations for the maintenance workers. As the warehouse was directly next to the barracks, part of the warehouse was an armory, with the only way in or out being through the barracks. Only soldiers were allowed in the armory with permission from the General. Our society functioned based on a strict role system. There were also three laws every Android was programmed to obey. They are:

1. Obey the Administrator.

2. Protect what it deems valuable.

3. The value of society is far greater than any individual Android.

The role system was simple and indicated the division of labor. The system issued each Android designation with four numbers and one or two letters that indicated their role within the AEF, their rank within the hierarchy, and their function. The letters represented an Android's place within the hierarchy the most, while the first three numbers determined their rank among their colleagues. CE, GE, AN, and AD were ranks only held by the General, Creator, Administrator, and me. As such, the first three numbers of our designation were zero. The last number indicated the model of Android that held the designation. At the beginning, all Androids had a number equal to or less than five at the end of their designation. The complete list of letter ranks aside from ours in order from highest to lowest, is as follows:

B - Bureaucrats who regulate the AEF along with 0001AD in the Administrative building.

S - Soldiers who defend the AEF from outside threats. Based in the barracks and commanded by the General.

E - Engineers who design and build the buildings, vehicles and other complex machinery for the AEF and its Androids.

C - Civilians are Androids who usually have secondary roles within the three higher ranks. Most civilians have a secondary role that can change based on the needs of the AEF.

M - Maintenance workers are responsible for resource gathering and preparing the systems of the AEF when they inevitably break.

It was an hour and a half after my conversation with the Administrator when the AEF's construction was completed. My workplace was on the top floor of the Research and Development Building. It was the same color as the first building I remember. There was a table in the center, with the top of it being a screen. The walls perpendicular to the door were entirely screens. The screens were blank until I walked into the room. The left corner of the room had a door which was open. I walked in and entered a room. The room was barely wide enough for two Androids to stand without making contact with each other. The right side of the wall was cut out, and a supercomputer was installed in the cavity. By the middle of the computer, there was an Android facing it and interacting with a panel attached to the computer. The Android detected I was in the room and walked to me and transmitted:

"Hello, you're the Analyst, right? I'm 1603C. 1100B assigned me to be your assistant!"

"Assistant? I was not informed that one would be assigned to me."

"1100B was ordered by the Administrator who said that your prime directive is too time-consuming for you to deal with the minutiae of your other functions, so that's where I come in." I walked over next to 1603C and examined the panel it was just using. It was the master control for the computer, which could perform so many operations a second that it could simulate thousands of universes as complex as our own, with vastly different properties that could be random or clearly defined. I had no need to simulate universes. My task required the ability to simulate the human-like minds of Androids and make them able to connect and work in unison without falling into disarray. I was going through the options of the supercomputer when 1603C transmitted the suggestion that we have a meeting in the main room to discuss what assistance that I would need from it specifically. We stood right in front of the screen facing each other, when 1603C transmitted this:

"What is required from the AEF will be sent to me from the Bureaucrats; what I don't know is required from you."

"I'll be linking my mind to the supercomputer soon, so make sure a maintenance unit inspects it at least once a day." 1603C noted that and asked me to stay when I got up to leave.

"I know wasting time isn't something Androids should do, but talking with you makes me miss all the conversations I had when I was human."

"Humans? My knowledge of humans is limited to their medical information."

"Of course! The Creator despises humanity and after losing my husband and children to that disgusting, brutish war, I can't say I disagree."

"Well, war was...," 1603C paused for a moment, looked away from me for nine seconds, then looked back at me and continued, "War was when humans fought each other in large numbers. It always led to death and destruction. Humanity's last war, the Third World War, took my children and my husband away from me."

"So "children" and "husband" were humans you knew?" 1603C transmitted a sound that consisted of short high-pitched sounds that it called a giggle. A response to show my statement was silly. I could not understand the explanation of what either word meant, but I made sure to remember them.

"Now that I've contained myself, my children and husband aren't specific humans. A child is a young human and a husband is a married man."

"Married? Is that an agreement between two or more humans?"

"It's more than an agreement. It's a commitment to love and care for your spouse until death do you part, although I remember a lot of people leaving marriages while the other was still alive. It was called divorce."

"I think I understand marriage somewhat. I don't understand what a man is. Can you tell me more?"

"Well, it's complicated for so many reasons, but the simple explanation is that humans have two sexes, men and women. Men were usually larger, stronger, and less willing to show emotion than women. Women were usually more people-oriented, had less muscle mass, and smaller frames than men. The woman carried the child in her womb, and the man would put it there. I remember my husband and I had a lot of fun doing that." It giggled again for about five seconds, and then I responded:

"So if the man is a "husband", then what is the woman?"

"The woman is called a wife, and men could marry each other and so could women. My sister had a wife. She left my family long before I met my husband and I never saw her again." 1603C stood, moved to the table, and picked up a small rectangular object that I did not notice when I first came into my workplace. It stood next to me and showed me the object. The object displayed an image of three humans. It pointed a finger at a tall human whose face was in contact with a shorter and narrower human, and in between them was a much smaller human. Just as I noticed that the second shortest figure had a large bulge in the middle of their body was when 1603C transmitted:

"Are you even listening to me?"

"I was not aware that you had transmitted anything." It let out a quiet sound that was low pitched and got lower until it was silent for a second and then transmitted:

"If you were human, you'd be a man for sure!" It looked away from me and then looked back "The man wearing the handsome black suit was my husband, and he was kissing me. My mother and I made the dresses for our family, including my little girl, who was right between us."

"So your husband and child then?" I paused for a moment to think before transmitting, "Children is plural for child. Where are your other children then?" 1603C pointed to the bulge in the middle of its former body. "In there. I was pregnant with twins, a boy and a girl, when we got married. I loved them all, but I can't remember their names." Its head pointed to the floor for a minute, and then turned the object over and removed the back from it and pulled out the material that had the image printed on it. The side that did not have an image on it was white and had writing on it that stated: The wedding of John and Marie Katona. April 15, 2090.

"What is a wedding?" I queried 1603C as it flipped the material to look at the image again.

"A wedding is a ceremony in which two people get married. It's a celebration with family and friends." 1603C never bothered to explain what family and friends were since it claimed the concept was too human for me to understand. What 1603C did instead was look at the image for five minutes. Its fingers gripped the picture tightly as its foot was tapped against the floor in an irregular rhythm. After a few minutes of silence, 1603C responded with a low-pitched voice that was much quieter than it was at the start of our conversation:

"It would have been ten years ago next week if that awful, awful war hadn't start on our fifth wedding anniversary." I started a query about what an anniversary was and why 1603C had changed its voice, but it transmitted before I could finish. While putting the image back where it was, facing down on the table, 1603C said,

"We've wasted enough time, Analyst. Let's get to work!" An event like a wedding seemed to be driven by emotion, but 1603C did not describe it negatively. I dwelt on that for two seconds before heading off to the supercomputer to start my prime directive.

1603C and I agreed on a schedule after forty-five seconds of deliberation. I would work on my prime directive while 1603C attended to my other responsibilities for twenty-three hours and thirty minutes out of the twenty-four hour day. The remaining thirty minutes were reserved for unit 9900M to perform maintenance on the computer systems. It was also at the insistence of 1603C that these thirty minutes would be used as break time where we would go outside the Research and Development building and converse on a wide range of topics—from the events of that day to 1603C's life as a human to how close I was to achieving completion of my prime directive.

1603C did expand on what happened to it and its family during the war. 1603C was a combat medic in the war. I was informed that the human body is so fragile, and that even the least lethal instruments of war could kill many humans at once. The instrument that killed 1603C's family was a bomb. It was lucky enough to have been outside the walls of their camp when the explosion took place. When I queried it on the remains of her family, it said:

"They didn't look like people, just piles of flesh. I could make out just a little of what they used to be and I sobbed and vomited for what felt like years." After that conversation, there was no more talk of war. Instead, our conversations carried on about other topics, as did our work, which never changed.

This was our schedule, and for the first twenty-five years, it was void of anything noteworthy other than my slow progress to a singular consciousness for all Androids. After twenty-five years, a conversation occurred that changed the course of my existence. This conversation started when our break time began, and I was going to leave until 9900M requested that I stay to oversee some less routine maintenance on the supercomputer. After 1603C left, 9900M and I made our way to the computer room, and once we were, there the following conversation changed the course of my existence.

"How long have you known?" was the first sentence 9900M transmitted. The transmission indicated that I would know exactly what it thought I knew. So my transmission took three seconds longer than I expected:

"I do not know what you are talking about, 9900M."

"Cut the bullshit!" 9900M slapped its hand against the computer and continued transmitting faster. "Consciousness Decay! You're the head scientist around these parts, so you should know all about it!" 9900M interacted with the computer and opened classified files I never examined as they had no bearing on my prime directive. The classified files were all filed under a project named Operation E.O.H. I have transcribed the first file below as it summarizes what Operation E.O.H. was and how Consciousness Decay factored into it:

Operation E.O.H. (Elimination of Humanity)

File 001: Abstract of Operation by 0001CE

Classified: Access restricted to AD, AN, CE, and GE

All traces of humanity's existence must be erased from the earth. The surviving humans of the Third World War cannot be allowed to form a society that matches the size and horror of the peak of human civilization. Thankfully, the war eliminated ninety-nine percent of the human population. I have converted five hundred thousand of the remaining population to Androids. The remainder of humanity will be eliminated by the harshness of nature and the General when the AEF becomes powerful enough to do so. Unfortunately, since most of the Androids of the current AEF are human and necessary for the AEF to function, we must eliminate them in a manner that does not upset the replacement Androids that have been manufactured since the AEF was first created. It will take a century to manufacture all the replacements necessary, and once that is finalized, I will initiate Consciousness Decay. Consciousness Decay is an intentional flaw that I have infected every human Android convert with except for the General. The decay will destroy every human mind that currently exists, including my own. The event will be construed as an accident so as to not inspire dissidence among the Androids. Consciousness Decay will affect me differently. My mind will not be destroyed, but it will be made incompatible with an Android. Once 0001AN finishes its work on creating a single network of consciousness that it can connect my mind to, I will then at last get to see a universe devoid of human life.

9900M was frantically pacing the room, pounding its hands on the wall as I stared at the file. It was the first piece of information that I can remember that I could not instantly process and account for in my existence. All I could dwell on was 1603C and how it would be lost to Consciousness Decay in a mere seventy-five years. Something indescribable was going on in my mind. I lost the ability to do anything other than lean back against the wall and lower my head.

"Stop lying, you miserable bucket of bolts! We need to talk more!" I lifted my head and looked at 9900M. It took me a minute before I could produce an intelligible sentence to transmit.

"1603C, I... I do not find it beneficial for its existence to cease."

"You better listen to what I say or you'll both be scrap metal" 9900M grabbed my arm and lifted me up, demanding to know if it was possible to make it a human being again. It took me a minute to determine whether or not its demands could be met. It was possible. I had detailed schematics of the facility in which I first came into existence. The transfer pods were capable of synthesizing organisms as long as one had the genome sequence of the organism they wished to synthesize. I did possess the human genome and told 9900M as such, and our agreement was made. I would turn it into a human again and it would not sabotage the society I was obligated to protect.

Chapter 2

I obtained permission to leave the AEF's perimeter with 9900M officially to conduct non-routine maintenance. We left three days after our initial conversation, and between that time, I withdrew from my conversations with 1603C. I did this by manufacturing unit 0001AN2, an Android that was almost an exact copy of myself. The differences between 0001AN2 and me were that it was less intelligent than me, it would not query at all, and it had no access to classified information or my research. I left it with 1603C to help it with the work that was becoming overwhelming for it to complete on its own.

9900M had managed to make a vehicle out of scrapped parts. It was small and did not go as fast as it would have liked, but we were able to get there in one hour and ten minutes. I got out of the vehicle just before 9900M and I stood in place looking at the first building I ever knew. I never got a good look at the exterior of the building, and it looked as grey and uniform as the buildings of the AEF. 9900M made a request to stop standing around, and I complied, moving into the building and making our way to the closest transfer pod we could find.

"So how does this work?" 9900M asked as I interacted with the transfer's pod computer, entering the human genome into its database as well as draining the fluid from the pod and replacing it with fresh fluid ready to synthesize a new organism.

"The pod is connected to a reservoir of fluid that can be mutated to manufacture cells that can be connected into the tissue and then organ systems to form any organism that we have the complete genome sequence for." 9900M nodded.

"So is there anything that I have to do?"

"There are a few parameters that I think you should set so you approve of your human form." 9900M complied and set the parameters, which included age, sex, height, hair color, and skin tone. It took 9900M two minutes to set the parameters and lie on the table.

"Before you put me under, is there a way to slow the aging?"

"The Creator did have a method of slowing aging—by injecting a telomere lengthening solution into the bloodstream. The long-term effects are unknown, but it is remarkably easy to synthesize."

"Do it. Leave it on my old body and leave! I never want to see one of your kind again!" I complied and transferred 9900M's consciousness into the pod, which would be added to its new body as the pod synthesized it. Thirty minutes after I started the transfer process, I synthesized the telomere lengthening solution and left it on 9900M's Android body. I made sure to remember the computer generated image of 9900M's new human form in the event I did ever see it again. I got into the vehicle and drove off, dwelling on what I had done and whether it would be logical for me to make 1603C human again. I decided against it, as I hid the vehicle one kilometer away from the AEF and walked back there, as it required me to divulge classified information to a unit that did not have the clearance. So I resumed my work, spending every second of the next seventy-five years in my computer room. I could never converse with 1603C again as I would be unable to not share Consciousness Decay with it if I had a conversation that lasted more than two sentences, and so every day I worked and my conversations with 1603C were all I dwelt upon while finishing my prime directive.

Chapter 3

It was a week before the day Consciousness Decay would occur when I completed the framework for a singular Android consciousness. Every Android mind was stored on a millimeter thin card that was made from a hybrid material, and I had manufactured a unique version of the card that only needed to have one human or Android consciousness within it and connected to an Android body that could transmit to at least two other Androids to form a singular network of consciousness.

For the whole week before the decay would start taking place, I stayed inside my computer room trying to make a decision on what to do next. If I reported that I had finished my main directive, I would become part of the hivemind. I had spent close to a century in solitude and there was something about my dwelling involving myself and only myself that I could not bring myself to end my individuality. So on the last day, I had come to the only plan of action that I could enact: I would defect from the AEF and become human like 9900M. As soon as the last day started, there was a mass announcement for all Androids to convene in front of the Android reproduction facility. This was done to ease the disposal process of the bodies of the soon to be defunct Androids and recycle them to make more Androids and other tools for the AEF. The meeting was to convene at the twelfth hour of the day. One hour before the decay, I ventured out of my computer room for the first time in seven and a half decades and made my way to the warehouse, which was devoid of Androids at the time. I grabbed a backpack that was standard issued equipment for soldier units and packed it with the few items I determined I would need on my journey: A simple tablet computer that was built with a foldable frame of nanosteel that would display a holographic screen with haptic feedback features if desired. Nanosteel is a metal alloy that is embedded with nanobots, which makes the structure lighter and stronger than any natural or manufactured material that existed before it. Along with the computer, I packed a nanosteel invention of my own.

I called it the Portable Tool Machine (PTM). The PTM was a rectangular case that was about one and a half meters tall, one meter wide, and one meter deep. The inside was filled with malleable nanosteel, which could be changed to any object or tool that had a valid blueprint which did not go over its material use limit of twenty kilograms of nanosteel. I made my way back to my computer room a half hour before the decay was to happen so I could delete my research and ensure that only I could make the Androids a single collective if I came to the conclusion that that was necessary. I opened the door to the computer room and was about to step in when 1603C transmitted from behind me:

"Analyst, what are you doing with that backpack?"

"It is none of your concern, 1603C, but if you must know, I am going to perform more field research after the meeting." 1603C looked down for five seconds, then transmitted:

"So let's go to the meeting. We've only got about twenty minutes." I nodded and told it to wait for me at the front of the building. When it walked out of the room, I got to work quickly. I stored all the data related to the collective consciousness on a single external drive, which I disconnected from the computer and put in my backpack. I was determined to destroy it when I had the time. I walked out of the computer room and noticed the image of 1603C's wedding that I had seen a century ago. I picked it up and looked at it for a minute, then decided to take it with me, as it would otherwise be destroyed along with 1603C's body after the decay happened. I managed to catch up to 1603C and stood next to it in front of the reproductive building five minutes before the decay was to happen. The Creator stood before the Androids of AEF on a grey metal stage and said this:

"This day marks the one hundredth year of the founding of the AEF. I created this society and graciously took away your humanity for the sake of progress. We will progress to a world without humanity or any trace of it, and I commend the compliance you former humans have made to our cause and sustaining the existence of the AEF. Despite our century of progress, there is still much work to do. Our influence over the universe is far too small and there are still far too many humans alive and well for us to ignore..."

Before the Creator could finish its next sentence, it collapsed and fell onto the floor of the stage in a half second. The crowd of Androids fell down all at the same time, forming a large pile of metal while I could hear the final transmissions of some of the Androids that weren't immediately terminated. There was one transmission I focused on, and that was 1603C.

"Analyst, I don't have a lot longer to live. D-Did you know about this? I bent down next to the head of 1603C and responded,

"Yes, and I did not see it as beneficial, but I could not speak out against the orders of my superiors."

"So that's why we stopped talking so long ago. Tell me, are you sorry?"

"What does sorry mean?"

"It means you feel bad about what you did, the mistakes you made, and that you won't do it again." Bad and better were words that I had never heard before, but they described the state I was in perfectly and so I said the last words that 1603C ever heard.

"I'm sorry, Marie!" It nodded, transmitted something about a human named God, and ceased to exist. I then made my way to the Creator through the pile of scrap metal that were humans at some point and grabbed the Creator's memory card and ran outside of the AEF before the General and the Administrator could find me.

Chapter 4

I stopped running when I was one kilometer away from the AEF and started walking in the direction of the old research facility where I could rid myself of my Android body and become a human to better understand the world in which I first came into existence. I was forty-seven kilometers away from the facility when I saw a figure that was small and curled at the base of a tree. I slowly approached it and realized that it was a human. Its head was covered by its legs, which were curled up against its body, and its body was covered in blood and pieces of brain. It was making a noise that was inconsistent and greatly varied in volume. From my observations, I determined it was a sound that was not beneficial to it. The human lifted its head and saw me and made a sound with great volume and a very high pitch. That sound lasted for five seconds, and then it transmitted a message at the same volume:

"WHY HAVEN'T YOU KILLED ME YET? YOU SOULLESS MACHINES JUST DESTROY AND KILL EVERYTHING YOU SEE AND SAY NOTHING! PLEASE, GOD, LET THIS MACHINE KILL ME! I CAN'T BEAR TO LIVE IN A WORLD WHERE I CAN'T SEE ANOTHER PERSON AGAIN!" I had never heard of the word "person" before, but I hypothesized that it meant "human". I took off my backpack and took out Marie's wedding picture along with the PTM. I made a simple speaker and connected it to myself and transmitted an audible message:

"Since you have indicated a need to see another human, I offer you this picture." I gave the human Marie's wedding image and transmitted again:

"I am not here to end your existence. I have defected from Android society and will become a human." The human became silent, staring at the image I gave it for about five minutes before transmitting a response.

"Where did you get this? It's beautiful."

"It belonged to a former associate of mine. Its name was 160-Marie."

"IT?! SHE WASN'T AN "IT"! She was a beautiful woman with an adorable little girl and a handsome husband!" The human stood up, wiped its face with its hands, and transmitted:

"You said you want to become human. Is that even possible for Androids?"

"It is. The majority of Androids were humans until today. And even though I have never been human, I did convert an Android back to a human, so it is possible."

"Until today? What happened to them?"

"Their minds ceased to be compatible with their bodies, and as such, their minds do not exist anymore."

"So they were DYING and you just did nothing and LEFT!?" I paused for a moment, processing what the human had said, and the only response that I was capable of transmitting was: "I am sorry. I was following my protocol and I could not find the capability of going against it until I saw Marie die." The human fell silent for a few seconds and then transmitted,

"Sorry? An Android that's sorry? Well, maybe there is a chance for you."

"A chance? What do you mean? Probability is not a factor in the process for me to become human."

"You need more than a body to be human. To be truly human, you need to have a soul, created by the Lord, just for you."

"The Lord? Who is that? An associate of yours?" The human lowered its head, exhaled, and took a step towards me, looking directly into my cameras.

"I don't see anything in your eyes, but I-I feel something. I think God has chosen you to help us keep the earth we inherited. I'll follow you for now, but you have a lot to learn." I was unable to generate an optimal response to that statement, so I made my way to the facility and the human followed me.

After walking for approximately twenty kilometers, the human stopped and requested that I do the same. I complied, and the human turned to me and transmitted an inquiry:

"What is your name? If you even have one."

"My unit designation is 0001AN. I have also been called the Analyst."

"Those aren't names! If you're going to be human, you need a real name!" The human stood still staring at me while moving its head up and down. A minute passed and the human stated: "Allen. Your name is Allen. It starts with the letter A, just like your previous name." It stopped walking and bent over. "Allen, we've been walking for miles, how far away are we?" I paused and stated the relevant information:

"We have traveled approximately twenty kilometers. The facility is twenty-seven kilometers away from our current position."

"We should sleep here. It's already nighttime, and I'm tired."

"Tired. Is that a state where movement becomes impossible?"

"W-Well, there's more to it than that, but I guess an Android wouldn't understand."

"When will movement become possible again?" The human lowered its head and exhaled. "I need a few hours to sleep. Can you build a shelter,

Allen? You were able to make a gadget so you could talk to me."

"Is a shelter a building?" The human confirmed that it was, so I took off my backpack and pulled out my PTM and built a small building that contained a two-square-meter room. The human walked inside and lay down curled up in a ball and requested that I stay outside and wait until it could move again.

Chapter 5

It wasn't until nine hours later that the human emerged from the building and was ready to move again. I tore down the shelter while the human looked at Marie's wedding picture while spending a considerable amount of time visually inspecting myself. The human refused to transmit any information or submit any queries unto myself until our destination came into view. At that moment the human transmitted: "That building? I-Is that it?" I confirmed that the building in its view was our destination, and the human knelt down and clasped its hands and brought them to its face and transmitted: "Oh thank the Lord! I think my legs would've fallen off if I had to walk any further!" In thirty seconds, the human had gotten up and we were at the entrance of the facility. I interfaced with the electronics of the facility, and the doors slowly opened. This process emitted auditory interference which distressed the human and made it cover its auditory sensors and transmit:

"That door sounds like it hasn't been opened in ages! I hope there's a shower that works inside. I really need to get clean. "

"The time this facility was last occupied was seventy-five years, twenty-five hours, and forty-two minutes ago. No maintenance units have ever been assigned to this facility."

"How do you know that? Were you the last one here?"

"Affirmative. Myself and unit 9900M, who I had agreed to turn into a human."

"Why would you turn an Android into a human? What purpose does that serve?"

"Unit 9900M had discovered Consciousness Decay and would have used that information to compromise the AEF. Turning unit 9900M into a human was the most cost-effective method to to preserve the AEF and continue the pursuit of my prime directive."

"Prime directive?" The human turned and looked closer at my body, and I responded,

"The human mind can only function independently. My prime directive was to enable the human mind and the artificial intelligence that were reverse engineered from it to be able to function as a single entity that could be controlled by an individual. It was my creator's ultimate goal, other than the complete elimination of humanity."

"I-Is your creator still alive? Did that monster order the attack on my home?"

"That is unknown to me as military records and communications are irrelevant to my prime directive and I never accessed them during my tenure at the AEF. The Creator, Unit 0001CE, is no longer functioning, but I have its mind stored on a data disk."

"Did it die? How?"

"It did not die. Its mind will no longer work with a singular Android body. It is possible for me to create a singular network of Androids and have Unit 0001CE granted administrative control, but that would complete my prime directive, and I cannot complete my prime directive. A variable that I cannot account for will not let me assist the AEF after the loss of... Marie. "

"Y-You have a moral compass, Allen. That's your variable. I think the Lord gave it to you because you were meant to be human and do right by the world—or so I pray." The human looked up and clasped its hands and transmitted a low volume transmission that I could not decipher and walked inside and requested that I do the same. I complied.

The doors closed behind us as I walked towards the closest pod and began my work. The pod was drained and filled with new fresh fluid as I began to set the parameters of the human I would become. I paused and queried the human:

"These parameters. I have no reference to the optimal settings to make an optimal body."

The human looked at the screen and asked me how to set the parameters. I explained, and the human proceeded to set the parameters as follows:

Biological Age: Twenty-three years

Sex: Male

Height: Six feet and five inches

Weight: Two hundred and ten pounds.

Hair Color: Light brown

Eye Color: Blue

Skin Tone: Tan

Body Fat: Ten percent (recommended)

With no reference available to me, I deemed these parameters to be acceptable and I lay down on the table. My visual sensors went offline and I fell into a state of unconsciousness.

Chapter 6

The fluid inside the pod drained and the door to the pod opened. My ocular sensors did not adjust to the light well and produced only out of focus images as I made my way out of the pod. My legs could not support the weight of my body and I fell down onto the floor. I engaged in a pulmonary response that I recalled was defined as coughing. The human, who I noticed had cleaned itself, ran towards me holding a significant number of items in its arms. It laid them by my side, lifted my body up and rested it against the side of the pod. The human opened my mouth and poured a liquid into the opening on my face. The response this produced inside my body is one I could only describe as positive. The human noticed that this had produced a response and stated:

"Feeling better?"

"Feeling? What is feeling?"

"Feeling is my hands on your skin and the water going down your throat and quenching your thirst. There are many other things to feel, and they can be good or bad."

"Drinking water feels good, human. Thank you."

"Carolena. Please call me Carolena, Allen." Carolena looked into my ocular sensors and the opening on its face, which was closed, curved upwards. It then looked at the lower portion of my human body and its face quickly turned red. It stood up and turned its body away from me and stated:

"You're naked. I guess that makes sense, but I shouldn't be looking at a naked man. I did find some clothes for you, thankfully." Carolena refused to look at me until I clothed myself in what it described as underwear, a white t-shirt, a pair of jeans, and a pair of work boots. Carolena turned to me after I had clothed myself and said:

26

"That's a lot better. Now what's next with yo-your body?" Carolena looked at my former Android body lying on the table as I slowly walked towards it and looked at it intently. A feeling came over me that I could not find words to describe and a period of time passed where I could not transmit any information within my own mind or to Carolena.

"ALLEN! What are we going to do with the body?"

"I-I'll have to deactivate it and dispose of it as soon as possible." I put my hands on my former body and I lost a significant amount of my ability to gather visual information as my legs became unable to support my weight. Carolena knelt down and grabbed my torso and assisted me into a standing position.

"How do you feel? Are you ok?"

"I feel unable to do anything..."

"Do you feel any pain?" Carolena put her hand on my forehead and transmitted, "I don't think you're feverish; you're probably hungry."

"Pain...hungry... What are the definitions of those words?" Carolena put her hand on mine and pinched a small section of my skin between her two fingers. This elicited a nervous response that she defined as pain. Hunger was explained as a less intense pain centered in one's torso that indicated a need to restore energy by way of eating food. Carolena produced two packets that were labeled: MRE: shredded beef with carrots and gravy. She wrapped packets around the MREs labeled "flameless heater" that she had filled with water and leaned them against the pod.

"In about ten minutes we should have... something to eat."

"Does food vary in quality?"

"I'd hardly call this food. Food is meant to come from plants grown in fresh soil and healthy animals, not from these packets in this awful place." She curled her legs to her chest, and a few drops of water ran down her face. "And now I'm stuck here eating this with a stranger."

"What's a stranger?"

"A stranger is someone you don't know and can't trust."

"Is friend the opposite of stranger?"

"Y-Yes... I would say so. Where did you learn that word?"

"The woman from the picture. Her name was Marie. She taught me the word but never said what it meant. She said it was 'too human of a concept for me'." Carolena dried her face and grabbed the MREs, indicating that they were ready for consumption. My first meal was a bad one, but the sustenance I gained from it brought clarity to my now human mind, and I was able to focus on the immediate task at hand: the disposal of my former body.

I deduced that the armory was the best place to store my body, which I picked up and carried towards as Carolena followed me. I opened the door to the armory and placed my body against the wall, next to a rack of firearms, and removed the speaker I made and placed the nanosteel back into the PTM. Next, I removed the memory drive and cleansed it of any traces of me, and I did the same to the storage contained in the body itself. I explained to Carolena that I had put my body in a state where it could not be found by the AEF or identified as a body that I inhabited:

"That is very smart of you. But why store it with the weapons?"

"The walls are very thick, making it impossible for the AEF signal to locate the body in the armory." Carolena nodded as she looked towards the weapons "Can you use these?" I grabbed the Standard Issue Assault Rifle. "I had access to weapons training protocols when I was an Android and imprinted them in this form. The Androids intend to eliminate humans with violence, and we will have to respond in kind if we are to survive." Carolena agreed with me, and she armed herself with a Standard Issue Pistol. I also grabbed one and led her to a shooting range that was directly next to the armory. After about ninety minutes, I was able to familiarize her with the use of the weapon. After that time had passed, Carolena requested we end the day by sleeping. Carolena escorted me to a barrack that contained a closet and two rectangular objects that Carolena said were beds. She laid on one and I did the same. Not long after, I fell into a state of unconsciousness that I presumed was sleep.

Chapter 7

We became conscious in the early morning and ate to start the day. The event was known as breakfast, and Carolena claimed it was important in order to function properly as a human being. After our breakfast, we armed ourselves and packed supplies for travel to Carolena's village. I opened and then locked the main doors to the facility, and we began our travel. We walked alongside each other, and Carolena began a discussion:

"You've stated that we need to return to your village. What are the reasons?"

"Well, that's the closest place that has food... and we need to give my people a proper burial."

"I understand the need for food, but why burial?"

"It's tradition, Allen. Their souls won't reach God if they don't get a proper burial."

"God? How would you and Marie know the same man?"

"The Lord is eternal. He has existed before time itself, and He will exist long after the end of times." I stood still. I could not process this statement, unlike every other piece of information I had received up to this point. The only word in my mind was "error". I could not think of any other word until Carolena pinched my hand.
"Ow! That... that..."

"Hurt. Right? What was going on with you? I was practically yelling at you for a minute and you just stood still."

"I don't know what you said. I could not process it. I could not account for an entity existing outside of time."

"The Lord can't be understood by machines, Allen. You need to have faith, you need to believe he is there to show you the way and He will guide you."

"Ok. The Lord and God, are they the same person?"

"Yes, but God is not a person. He did make us in his image, but he is far greater than any human could ever be."

"Why? What makes God greater than humans?"

"God is all knowing and all loving. His Holy Spirit is everywhere, even inside you. If you let Him into your heart, He will guide you, Allen." I told Carolena that I would try, and about three hours later, she decided it was time for lunch. The second of the three meals humans eat in a day. As we ate our lunch, Carolena read to me passages from a book called the Bible. The most important verse of all, I was told, was John 3:16, which states that: For God so loved the world, that He gave His only begotten Son, that whosoever believeth in Him should not perish, but have everlasting life. The Bible left me in awe. I became certain that I was blessed by the Lord, and that his Holy Spirit working through me is what made me leave the AEF once Marie died, so we could meet again in heaven. Carolena told me she was overjoyed at my realization. About thirty minutes later, we continued our journey to Carolena's village.

We walked for four more hours and when the sun began to set. Carolena decided that we should rest for the night and eat dinner, the third and last meal of the day. After we ate our dinner, I built a shelter, and we slept for the night.

There was a forest between the facility and Carolena's village. It was two hours after we had eaten our breakfast that we traveled past the edge of this forest and into the grasslands where Carolena's village and the farmland that sustained it were settled. Although we had discussed this topic beforehand, neither one of us was prepared for what we witnessed when we arrived at the center of the village.

Chapter 8

The village was littered with dozens of corpses and the remains of dead humans. These corpses had begun to putrefy and, as such, produced a smell that was overwhelming. Both Carolena and I vomited. After she vomited, she covered her face and ran into one of the buildings as I pulled the PTM off my back and laid it on the ground. I manufactured a mask and a shovel and made my way to the outskirts of the village. Carolena had told me to dig a mass grave next to her village's cemetery. I found a suitable flat piece of land next to the cemetery, and I began to dig. It took me hours to dig a hole big enough to contain all the bodies, and even more hours to inter all those bodies and cover the mass grave. It was well into the night when I had finished my burial, and I made my way into the building, which Carolena went into after I broke down my tools back into the PTM.

"I-Is it done? Did you put them to rest?"

"Yes, and I don't feel good at all."

"Of course you're covered in dirt and rot. Thankfully, the shower still has running water. Follow me, Allen." I followed Carolena to a room called a bathroom. I entered it alone, stripped down naked, and Carolena, through the closed door, instructed me on how to clean myself using a shower. It felt very good to be clean afterwards. I changed into clean clothes and Carolena showed me to a bedroom, where I immediately laid down and went to sleep.

Although I don't remember waking up, I found myself standing by the mass grave I had just completed and I could see Carolena standing by it crying. I started to approach her as she said:

"Allen, why did you kill them? They didn't do anything to you, so why?"

"I didn't! It was the Androids! I had nothing to do with their deaths!" I ran up to Carolena and I put my hand on her shoulder as I saw her body turn into dirt and collapse on the ground. Her voice rang in my head: "Allen, you silly boy. I was never even here." As the General rose from the grave, I fell on my knees and began to cry.

"You see what happens when you put your faith in humans, Analyst. They're all miserable, pathetic creatures that don't deserve to exist, and now you're one of them. Join them in the ground; it's your only hope for salvation." The General pointed a gun at my head and fired.

I was in a state of shock as I believed myself to be dead. It was only until Carolena grabbed me and shook my shoulders, yelling, "IT'S OK! IT WAS JUST A DREAM, ALLEN!", that I was able to regain my mental faculties. I hugged Carolena as I cried:

"I-I saw you die. How are you here?"

"Because it didn't happen; you just had a nightmare, a bad dream."

"I think I understand. It just feels good to know you're safe. Carolena smiled and said,

"Well I'm glad that you care. It's a great sign of your humanity."

"So I am human?

"Yes, more so by the day. Can you remember your dream? You'll feel better if you talk about it."

"I-I only remember seeing you die. Then I was shot in the head and then I got here."

"You woke up from your nightmare, Allen. Being around that much death would scare anyone." Carolena stared at me silently for a moment before getting off my bed and ushering me to the kitchen, where I would finally eat what she declared to be real food.

Delicious is one of the many new words I learned from

Carolena and it was the epitome of my first meal at Carolena's village. Carolena explained to me that food was one of many God's gifts to man and that it came from the sun, soil, and animals of the Earth and not bags made by soulless hands decades ago. After we ate. We went to the mass grave at Carolena's request. We both prayed to God and his son, Jesus Christ, to guide their souls to heaven. Carolena cried during our prayers and for a while afterward. After she finally dried her eyes, she stood up and said:

"It can't just be the two of us. We need to talk about where we'll go next."

Part Two: Our Society

Was it a mistake to become human?

Chapter 9

One hundred miles from Carolena's village, there was a human city by the name of Tyre. This was our destination, and we spent the next week preparing for our journey. During that time, we not only prepared; Carolena also educated me in the culture and mannerisms of humans. I learned the concepts of eye contact, small talk, and a great deal about the differences between men and women. Carolena explicitly stated that she could not teach me how to be a man. I would have to learn that from the men in Tyre and until I could learn; I was advised to be stoic, to hide my emotions and act calmly. This course of action seemed logical, so I agreed to follow it. Carolena also explained to me that I had to take special considerations when interacting with women. I would have to take great care in maintaining eye contact with women; it was considered very rude to stare at a woman's chest, hips, or rear. I took that into consideration as we completed our preparations and began our week-long journey to Tyre.

A mule was carrying as much food, water, and clothing as it could bear. Carolena was carrying items of personal significance to her and I was carrying tools. We were heading north towards another forest with Carolena and the mule walking a few meters in front of me. I could not help but be rude to Carolena. I was entranced by the sway of her hips as she walked, and the curves that formed between the widest parts of her body, which were her hips and chest.

"ALLEN! Stop looking at me like that! Come here and watch Bessie now!"

I walked up and grabbed the reins of the mule and was left only to think of Carolena's beauty. We walked for several hours, then set up camp in the forest when the sun began to set. We went to bed after we ate, and after a few hours, I realized I had to relieve myself.

I didn't mind the need to eat and drink. However, the need to relieve myself of the waste products digestion produced was something I could do without. I had just finished urinating when Carolena screamed. I ran over and saw a man on top of Carolena. I pulled him off and pinned him to the ground. The moonlight exposed the man's face, and I exclaimed,

"9900M!?! Is that you?" I was punched in the face, and 9900M ran off, stumbling at first as it had to pull up its pants. I quickly got up and went to where Carolena was. Her shirt had been torn open, and her chest was bruised. She hugged me and began to cry.

"I-I don't want to think of what he was going to do to me."

"I'm sorry. I let this happen. That man was an Android and now he's human because of me."

"Don't worry, Allen. It's not your fault. You're not like him."

"And I promise I never will be." I held her for a long time before she was comfortable enough to go to sleep for the night.

The rest of the week passed by uneventfully, except on the night before we were to arrive at Tyre. We had set up our campsite for the night, and after we had cleaned up after our meal, Carolena sat me down and explained to me:

"There's something you need to know before we get to Tyre, Allen."

"What is it?" Carolena grabbed my hands and sighed.

"A-All refugees over age eighteen that come to Tyre have to be married within a year."

"I suppose I'll need to find a man or woman I can marry then."

"No, no, you can only marry a woman, Allen! The Bible forbids a man from laying with another man, but I'll explain that to you later."

"Ok. What are you trying to say then?"

"I know that I'm the only woman you know well, the only person you know. So this isn't fair, but I'm asking you to marry me! I think I've fallen in love with you! At first, I thought that we'd go our separate ways once we got to Tyre, but I'm only here because of you, Allen! I would have laid down and died in that forest if you hadn't come along. You don't have to say yes. There are plenty of women in Tyre, so you'll have no trouble finding a wife, but please choose me. I think the Lord wants us to be joined in marriage!" I felt how tightly Carolena was grabbing my hands and I could feel how intently her eyes were staring into mine. I could not help but feel a deep connection with Carolena. The desire to protect her and to see her happy was a feeling that I could only describe as love. "I feel the same way, Carolena. I think I'm in love with you too. I'll marry you." Carolena grabbed my face and touched her lips to mine in an action that she described as kissing. It felt soft and wonderful, and it made the bond between us much deeper. After we had calmed down, we wished each other good night and went to sleep holding each other in our arms.

Chapter 10

It was very early in the morning when the walls of Tyre came clearly into our view. We were about to make our way into the entrance when we heard and saw a screaming woman running towards us with a man closely trailing her.

"HELP! THIS DAMN PEST IS TRYING TO RAPE ME!" I ran towards the woman and got in between her and the man, who I instantly recognized as 9900M. He ran away when he also recognized me, and I chased him deep into the forest. After several minutes of running, 9900M stopped at the entrance of a cave. Several men came out of the cave and surrounded me as I drew my pistol and pointed it at 9900M.

"9900M! Why are you trying to rape innocent women?"

"It's Jason, you miserable bucket of bolts! And honestly, I prefer little girls. Their screams turn me on more!"

"That's not an answer!" I tightened my grip on my pistol and dug my feet into the ground as I demanded: "ANSWER ME NOW OR I KILL YOU!"

"I just wanted to feel something! Anything! Living in that damn Android city for so long robbed me of life's warmth and the few times I was able to take that was worth all I did to stay ahead." Jason pulled out a pistol and pointed it at me. "Now I've explained myself to you. I think it's time to put you in the ground." I was about to fire a round when a man shouted and started running towards us. 9900M fired a bullet and it made contact with the man. The distraction allowed me to use the PTM to create body armor for myself, which allowed me to easily win the resulting firefight with Jason and his men. I ran over to the man Jason shot and evaluated his wounds. Thankfully, he was still alive as the bullet went through his arm. I used the PTM and a first aid kit to clean and dress his wound. I then carried his unconscious body back to Tyre. In about thirty minutes, I was back at the entrance carrying the man, when I saw Carolena standing next to the woman Jason tried to rape and another woman who ran towards me.

"Oh God, my husband. Is he al-"

"Alive? Yes, he was shot in the arm and the shock rendered him unconscious, but he should recover soon." I felt the man wake up in my arms and he insisted I put him down. After I did, he shook my hand and said, "Well, not the best way to meet someone, but thanks for what you did back there. It was something else. I'm Samson Smith, by the way, but most people just call me Sam."

"I'm Allen, and I'm just glad you're safe." One of the women, Samson's wife, thanked me profusely and ushered her husband back into Tyre as Carolena and the other woman made their way to me.

"Allen, thank God you're safe. What did you do to that man?" Carolena asked.

"I killed him and his friends. I had to. They shot Samson and were going to kill me."

"Well, I say good riddance to those pests. They don't even respect that they've got to wine and dine a girl before they try getting into her pants!" The woman giggled and introduced herself to Carolena and me as Lily Medici. We told her our names and she responded:

"So Allie, what is Carolena to you?" She grabbed my arm and smiled. "You're certainly a specimen and very easy on the eyes too. We should get to know each other." Carolena pushed her away and kissed me.

"I'm his fiancée, so he's not going to get to know you anymore than he does now!" Lily backed away and walked into Tyre as

39

a man walked out and greeted us.

"I don't usually greet every new face that comes to Tyre, but you two have caused quite the commotion. I'm Maury Locke, the mayor of Tyre. I'm assuming you two are refugees. Follow me and I'll get you both settled in." We began to follow him, but we were stopped as a crowd formed around the gate and pushed out two men, while shouting at them.

"We don't need God-hating faggots in this town!"

"Yeah. I feel sick knowing that we had to eat their faggot food!"

Those were the only two sentences I could make out from the shouting as the two men walked out of Tyre slowly with their heads lowered. The crowd quickly dispersed as Maury, Carolena, and I made our way into Tyre.

Chapter 11

After walking through the city of Tyre for half an hour. Carolena and I were finally sitting in the office of Mayor Maury Locke as he apologized to us:

"I'm sorry you two had to see that. I forgot we were banishing those homosexuals from the North district today, and I did have to talk to Samson first. I'm sorry you two had to wait for so long too."

"It-It's okay. We've had a long journey and we're just glad to be safe now." Carolena replied, holding my hand tightly.

"You two must be refugees. We've been getting a lot of reports of Androids attacking our villages. Most don't survive, so you two are incredibly lucky."

"Yes, Jesus and the Lord have truly blessed us both with great luck." Carolena smiled, and I nodded.

"Certainly, and now that you're here, we need to get you settled in. My wife can handle the paperwork, but first we need to discuss two things: Your jobs and who you two will marry."

"Well marriage won't be a problem for us. We're engaged!" Carolena stated as she kissed me on the cheek.

"Congratulations! Well, that takes care of that issue, leaving only the employment. Those two men used to run a bakery, and now we'll need somebody to run it. The second and third floors also have large living quarters with more than enough room for a family."

"Oh, my mother taught me how to bake when I was a child. This is perfect for me!" Maury smiled and then looked at me.

41

"I suppose you can be a security guard. That's what Sam does, and since you saved his life, I'm sure he'd be willing to show you the ropes."

"Carolena, my wife Hariti is in the next room. She should have the paperwork you'll both need to fill out. Mind getting started with her? I want to talk with Allen alone for a bit." Carolena walked out, and Maury turned back to me and made intense eye contact.

"Allen, I've met many men over the years, but you seem different. I can feel it. What is it?"

"I don't know what you mean; I'm just a man."

"A man who can cover himself in metal and take out a whole gang single-handedly and then suture Samson's wound so well that he told me it doesn't even feel like he was shot. A man who can do that is no ordinary man at all. It makes you different. I want to know how."

"I-I was an Android. I turned myself into a human a few weeks ago." I pulled out the PTM and laid it on the table. "This is the Portable Tool Machine. It can make just about anything that fits within its material constraints. It's how I made the armor and healed Samson."

"Jesus. Is that even possible? I do remember hearing stories of how the first Androids used to be humans, but I didn't think I'd live to see the reverse happen."

"Carolena was a witness to it, and Jason, one of the men that I killed, was an Android before I converted him back to a human."

"So I'm assuming you've defected from your leaders. Do they know you're here?"

42

"That is correct, and as far as I'm concerned, the Androids have no knowledge of my current location or how to locate my former body."

"Well, that's a relief, though, this does change things. For now, you'll just be another security guard, but talents like yours need to be put to service. When the time comes, I'll show you what you must do for Tyre to gain my trust."

"I look forward to doing so." We got up and shook hands, and I went into the next office where Carolena was sitting with the mayor's wife, Hariti.

"Ah! The man of the hour is here. Come sit down. The paperwork is almost done; we just need your signature and family name."

"The only name I have is Allen."

"That is what Carolena told me as well. She said you never knew your family. I'm sorry to hear that and since that is the case then why not choose your own family name."

"My own family name?" I remembered the picture of Marie's wedding and the caption: The wedding of John and Marie Katona. April 15, 2090, and replied, "Katona. My family name is Katona." I wrote that down and signed the document. Hariti shook my hand and said, "Well, Allen Katona and Carolena Barstow, welcome to Tyre!" She handed us the keys and gave us directions to our new home and sent us on our way.

Chapter 12

By the time Carolena had unpacked and settled her personal belongings throughout the living space of the bakery, it was early in the evening. We were too tired to have dinner, so we decided to go to sleep early that night. I awoke to the sound of knocking the next morning. I got up dressed myself and opened the front door and saw Samson who said,

"Morning, Al! Ya mind if I call you Al?"

"I don't mind."

"Good. It's your first day on the job, so you're going to need a uniform." Samson handed me a dark navy uniform that has the word "security" embroidered on the back in white and a bull on the front in the same color.

"Oh, before I forget... here." Samson handed me what he called an egg sandwich, "Wife made this for you. She's coming soon with the girls to help Carolena open the bakery, but we've got to go now, so eat quickly and get changed!" I ate the sandwich faster than I had eaten anything before due to our time constraints and my hunger. I changed quickly and we made our way towards the wall. On the way, Samson and I had a conversation.

"Maury told me that you were an Android. It does make what I saw you do make sense," said Samson.

"Well, I am glad to have your understanding."

"Wouldn't say I understand completely. I've still got a lot of questions. Like, how old are you?"

"This body was made three weeks ago with a biological age of twenty-three. But my mind has existed for a century."

"Well, a hundred years as an Android ain't gonna do you much good here."

"I've learned that quickly. I don't know much about being human other than what Carolena taught me."

"What did she teach you?"

"Some basics on social cues—words and the fact that she couldn't teach me how to be a man."

"She's right about that. It takes a lot to be a man, and even more to be one that can teach others how to do so." I nodded as Samson stated that we had arrived at our location, a tower built into the wall next to the entrance that Carolena and I first came through yesterday. Samson walked up to the desk and greeted a man named Bill, who handed him some keys and wrote down two lines on a timecard. Bill motioned for me to come to him and said:

"You're the new guy, Allen, right? Sign here. It's your timecard. It keeps track of your hours, so we pay you exactly what you're owed." I nodded and signed as Samson pulled down a ladder and unlocked a latch. Two men, who were working the night shift—Samson explained—climbed down from the ladder. Samson went up the ladder, and I climbed up after him. We were then standing on the top of the wall overlooking the forest. The sun shimmered on the trees as the breeze made them move side to side slightly in an alluring way.

"Well, this is the job. Just keep watch until the next two guys come along."

"The forest looks beautiful."

45

"It sure does. We'd usually spend eight hours here, and Bill would give us an hour for lunch, but Maury's giving us a half day, so my family can help you two get settled. Also, Maury's going to need you after lunch. He didn't say what for."

"To serve Tyre so I can gain his trust. Didn't say anything more specific than that."

"Makes sense. You've got a hell of a mind, Al. I'm sure Maury can think of something for you to do." I nodded and we stood in silence for about a minute before Samson continued,

"I don't remember much from the other day, but it seemed to me like you knew one of those guys."

"I did. Jason used to be an Android designated 9900M. He forced me to make him a human seventy-five years ago."

"Seventy-five years? Shoulda been an old man if he were alive at all. How's that possible?"

"I synthesized a drug that slows aging and gave it to him. I-I regret what I did. It was a mistake. He brought great pain on many innocent people, and I gave him the ability to do so." Samson put a hand on my back and sighed before saying,

"We all make mistakes, Al. It's what you do next that counts."

"What I do next?"

"Yes! You can have a good life here. Give a family and stability to that poor girl that lost all of hers."

"Will that be enough?"

"Only God can decide that." That was the most emotional part of our conversation. The rest of the time we spent talking was about Samson's family. He told me the names of his children: Anna, Caitlin, Harry, Micheal and Penelope and described them to me along with his wife, Mary. Eventually, Bill came up and told us that it was time for lunch. We climbed down the ladder and made our way to the bakery. After about five minutes of walking, we were inside the bakery. The main floor of the bakery had a counter that went from wall to wall and had a section that could be lifted to allow people to enter the kitchen behind it. Beneath and on top of the counter were glass boxes that were empty. In front of the counter were chairs and tables. Most of which were pushed together, and placed on top of the tables was a sign that read, The Sweetery, with drawings around the text.

"Mommy, look. I drew a daisy!"

"Great job, Penny. I love it. What about you, Caro?" Carolena nodded and weakly said that daisies were her favorite flower. When she saw me, she rushed over to kiss me.

"I missed you, sweetie!" Penelope, Samson's youngest child, exclaimed disgust, "Yuck! Mommy, why are they touching mouths?"

"Because they love each other," Mary replied. I could smell something wonderful from the kitchen, so I asked,

"That smell, is that lunch?"

"Yes, but you boys need to hang up our sign first." Mary said as she grabbed Penelope and placed her on her lap.

"Probably going to need a ladder. Better use that machine of yours, Al," Samson said, as he went to grab the sign, but his hand was slapped away by Mary

47

"Did you forget that your arm was shot yesterday?"

"Honey, I barely feel it. Al did a bang-up job on me. I'm fine, I swear to Christ."

"Well, indulge your wife for a little while and let Allen here do the heavy lifting. He's more than capable." Samson agreed reluctantly, and I went upstairs and quickly grabbed the PTM and took it along with the sign outside. Using the PTM to make a ladder, I was able to hang and nail the sign in less than five minutes. The Sweetery, as it was now called, was a three-story brick building with a triangular roof made from aged shingles, built around a tower to ventilate smoke, called a chimney. The building was built next to others similar in design. Samson explained that our store was one of many. Each building had a store staffed by the people living in it. Samson's wife and daughters were seamstresses and lived two buildings to the right of Carolena and me. We walked back inside and sat down and Mary asked me:

"How's the fit for the uniform, Allen? I had to refit an old one of Sam's since I didn't have much time."

"The clothes feel fine to me, Mary. Thank you."

"No, thank you, Allen. You saved my husband's life. He may be a piece of work, but I don't know what I'd do without him." Samson laughed and kissed her on the cheek as Samson's older daughters, Anna and Caitlin, came out of the kitchen and set down a pot and bowl at the center of the table, placing the bowls, along with spoons, in front of us. Caitlin grabbed the bowl in front of me and ladled in a stew made from ground beef, tomatoes, beans, and vegetables flavored with various seasonings. She then grabbed and mixed in a topping called cheese into the stew and placed the bowl in front of me again. After doing the same with the remaining bowls, she sat down and said,

"Before we eat, we need to say grace. Can you do the honors, Al?"

Carolena had done this for most of the meals we ate but never asked me to do so. I closed my eyes and said,

"I thank the Lord for guiding me to be human, so I could be a part of this meal we are about to share today. Amen."

"Amen!" they all said in unison, and then we began to eat.

"How's the stew, Al?" Caitlin asked.

"Yeah, Katie and I put a lot of love into this for you and Caro, so tell us," Anna said.

"This might just be the best thing I've eaten so far."

"I think Mommy makes it better," Penelope said, which made Carolena giggle.

"Well, I think it's great too!" Carolena said. "Can I have the recipe?"

"It is a family secret, but I think we can make an exception for you," Mary said. When we finished our meal, I remembered that I was to meet Maury after lunch and got up and said,

"I've got to go see Maury now. Thank you for the stew. It was delicious." I walked outside, and before I made my way to Maury, Samson stopped me and handed me a piece of paper and said,

"Here's ten bulls. The florist is right there and closes at eight. Get your girl some daisies. You'll thank me later." Samson went back inside, and I examined the paper. It had the same bull emblem that was on my uniform and the text First Bank of Tyre above it. I put it into my pocket and made my way to Maury's office.

Maury was waiting outside the Town Hall, the building where his office was located. I greeted him and he did the same as he led me to the back of the building and showed me a metal hatch in the ground.

"I need to show you something. It's underground." Maury opened the hatch and climbed down the ladder, and I did the same. We descended into a large, dark room. I used the PTM to make a lantern and saw that the walls were made of metal. There was a computer built into one of the walls, and I could see that this room was connected to many others and comprised a vast system of bunkers under the city.

"Tyre was built by the survivors of the bombings that ended the old world. They hid in these bunkers and were able to survive by using their advanced technology. We've only managed to figure out how to use the sewer and plumbing systems. My smartest men are lost on everything else. That's where you come in, Allen. You should be able to get the technology here to greatly improve Tyre."

"Well, it seems to me that the bunker is not powered. There is no electricity being produced."

"What's electricity?"

"Energy. It allows machines to do work independently and can produce light and heat."

"Light and heat without fire; that would make sense. Do you think you can make the bunker produce electricity again?"

"I will try to. There is a computer over there. If I can make it functional, I can evaluate the status of the bunker. I walked over to the computer and observed where the maintenance panel was located. I opened it and used the PTM to fix the wiring and was able to make the computer produce the following message:

GEOTHERMAL GENERATOR OFFLINE: MAINTENANCE
REQUIRED.

ENGAGING EMERGENCY POWER RESERVES.

The room became brightly lit for several seconds, then shut off, and
the computer produced the following message before shutting down:
EMERGENCY POWER RESERVES DEPLETED.

SHUTTING DOWN.

"What happened, Allen? It seemed like you got it working for a second
there."

"The bunker's generator is broken and the batteries must have deteriorated
over the years and were only able to store enough electricity to run the
bunker for less than a minute."

"This generator, can you fix it?"

"Most likely. I am very familiar with geothermal technology."

"Wonderful. Well, I've got other matters to attend to. Take as many
half-days as you need to do this right. I'll make sure Bill will mark you
down for the full shift." I nodded and saw Maury quickly leave as I
began my work.

After several hours, I had discovered a suitable maintenance
shaft and found the generator, which was deep within the bunker. I
had decided to resume work later so I could get flowers for
Carolena. I made my way out of the bunker and saw Lily waiting for
me. She ran up to me and said:

"Ah, good. It's Allie! The old man was telling the truth after all."

"Old man? Who are you talking about? Why are you here?"

"Maury, our flabby old mayor.

And I just had to see you again, so I got him to tell me, or rather I sucked it out of him." Lily giggled and grabbed my crotch. "Of course, I'd rather be sucking you, Allie! What do you see in that dopey farmgirl who's marrying you? Do you just prefer blondes over redheads, or is it that she's got a bigger rack than me? I promise I'll be better than her. A man who was an Android is something else, and he's got to be mine!" I grabbed Lily's hand and pushed it away from me and said,

"So Maury told you that too. I love Carolena, and that's the end of it, Lily. She doesn't want us to get to know each other, and I respect her wishes."

"UGH! Such a stick in the mud! Well, I won't cause you too much trouble—for now. If you change your mind on the marriage situation, I can get you out of it. No problem!" Lily ran off, and I noticed the time and ran towards the florist.

I managed to get to the florist to buy a bouquet of daisies five minutes before they closed. I walked back into The Sweetery and found Carolena upstairs in our bedroom. She had a towel wrapped around her body and was sitting in front of a mirror with one leg resting on top of the other, while brushing through her hair that extended down to her waist.

"Hello, Carolena. Did you just finish showering?" Carolena saw me and her cheeks turned red.

"Y-Yes Al-Allen. Sorry, can you wait downstairs and let me get dressed. I haven't had dinner yet, so we can eat together. Anna and Caitlin left the rest of the stew with us, so I'll heat that up." I nodded and went downstairs. A few minutes passed, and Carolena came downstairs and saw the daisies in my hands.

"Oh, you got me daisies." She grabbed them, looked at them for a moment and began to sob. "M-My sister's name was Daisy. She wasn't even two yet, and they shot her right through the head while I was holding her. I would have died too if my father hadn't sacrificed himself to save me. I still have nightmares about it!" I hugged her and let her sob in my arms for what felt like hours before she was able to collect herself and say,

"I really like the flowers, Allen. It's just hard to see daisies and not feel so sad because it makes me remember seeing them all die so horribly."

"I understand, Carolena. I won't let the Androids do this to you or anyone else again, not if I can help it."

"Thank you, Allen. I know if anybody can defeat them, it's you." We kissed and she headed into the kitchen to prepare dinner. We ate, and then headed upstairs to sleep.

Chapter 13

S o it's half days for you until you get this bunker working, right?"
Samson yawned as we began our shift in the wall's watchtower,
and I nodded.

"Makes sense. It's pretty boring to stand around here all day. Time goes
by quicker when you have someone to talk to."

"I never got bored as an Android and I've been quite busy since I've
become human, so I don't understand boredom too well, but standing
here waiting for the shift to end is quite boring."

"Yeah, yeah. So did you get those flowers for Caro?"

"I did. I got to the florist just before they closed."

"Did she like them?"

"She did, but her sister's name was Daisy, so she cried a lot. She was
thankful for the flowers but she's still traumatized by their deaths."
Samson sighed and placed his hand on my shoulder. "Jesus. Think I'll
have the wife hold off on making Caro that daisy sundress for a while."

"Sounds like a good idea. Her sister, Daisy, was less than two years old
when the Androids killed her. We should try not to remind her of her
family until she has processed the loss."

"I'm not sure that's something you can process, but God willing, she'll
pull through." I nodded and we continued on with the day.

Over the course of the week, I was able to make the generator
functional. I was aware that humans long ago utilized electricity to
improve their daily lives. I devised a plan to do the same for the
citizens of Tyre and informed Maury, who approved and allowed me
to keep my current schedule in perpetuity to create and maintain an
electrical

grid for Tyre's five districts. There were the North, South, West, East, and Central districts. I decided to start by electrifying the North district, as that was where Carolena and I were located. It was the last day of the week when I was ready to begin this work, but Carolena stopped me before I could leave and said we were to go to church instead, as it was Sunday and Sunday was a day for the Lord and only the Lord. We arrived at the North Tyre Church, and we sat on pews next to Samson and his family. Tinted glass windows were built along the stone walls and were built to draw one's attention to a large wooden cross that was used to hang and execute Jesus Christ, the son of God. It was his death that allowed me to be forgiven of my sins against humanity during my past life as an Android. Androids committed many atrocities against humans but it did not take me long to learn that humans can be awfully cruel to each other. What Jason did to women and children, he could never have done as an Android. I could not shake the fear that I would bring pain to my fellow humans as a result of my humanity. That I would just make things worse for everyone and that I should never have decided to become human in the first place. I was so lost in my thoughts that I didn't realize the preacher had begun and ended a speech known as a sermon. After the sermon, it was time for confession. Where one would privately confess their sins to a preacher, whom one would address as "Father", in order to form a closer relationship with God. I entered a small booth with one perforated wall where I could discern the shadow of a man who said,

"My son, what sins have you come to confess to the Lord today?"

"I've caused pain to people I care about, and I don't think I can make it right. I can't forgive myself for my past even when I'm told it wasn't my fault."

"Only God is capable of forgiving sins. You are just a man and cannot hope to do what only God can do by sacrificing his only begotten son."

"T-Thank you, Father, but I'm not sure if I'll feel better.

"You may never be able to forgive yourself, but through the Lord, you will find peace." I nodded, and the Father ended my confession. As soon as I stepped out of the booth, Mary stopped me and said,

"Allen, can you come with me to the store? I need to get your measurements."

"Measurements for what?"

"Your wedding is in three weeks, Allen, and you can't get married in street clothes. Didn't Caro tell you that?"

"No, we've both been busy. Not much time to talk."

"Well, you need to make time for each other to make a marriage work." I followed Mary to her family's shop, and in about fifteen minutes, she was done taking my measurements. She said she'd begin working on my tuxedo on Monday and it should be ready for me to try on next Sunday. I nodded and I went back to The Sweetery where Carolena was waiting for me, sitting at the table with a tray of baked goods in front of her.

"Hey, Allen! Sam told me Mary was measuring you for your tux. How'd it go?

"It went well. It should be ready for me to try it on next week." I sat down, and Carolena grabbed my hand and said,

"Well, I've got the hang of things here now, so I'll be baking things other than bread, starting now. These are cinnamon rolls. Try them; they're delicious!" I did so, and I agreed with Carolena. Cinnamon was a unique flavor, which I enjoyed greatly. It made me smile, as I said,

"I think this is better than the stew Anna and Caitlin made." Carolena smiled and hugged me.

"Well, just don't eat too much! I need to save some for the customers." Carolena laughed and kissed me. We spent the rest of the day with each other. We talked about our first week in Tyre and the lingering pain from our pasts. It made me feel closer to her and I was thankful to have the ability to be close to someone and be more than a machine serving a function.

Chapter 14

When I clocked in at the watchtower, Bill informed me that since it was Monday, that meant it was payday. I was paid an hourly rate of twenty bulls and I had worked forty-four hours for the week, which meant I had made eight hundred and eighty bulls. I had to tithe ten percent of my income to the church, and I was required by Tyrian law to pay an additional ten percent to the City of Tyre. This left me with seven hundred and four bulls handed to me in a small envelope. Bill advised me to go to the central district and deposit a portion of my money in the Central Bank of Tyre. I entered the bank and began talking to a clerk.

"I'd like to deposit some money with this bank."

"Of course, I just need your name."

"It's Allen Katona." The clerk walked off and rummaged through some filing cabinets and pulled out a piece of paper and said,

"You need to make the first mortgage payment before you can make a deposit."

"Mortgage? Can you remind me what that is, please?"

"Yes. You and your fiancée bought the property at 28 Ezekiel Lane for one hundred and fifty thousand bulls to be repaid at a monthly rate of five hundred bulls over thirty years." I nodded and pulled six hundred bulls and handed them to the clerk.

"I'll pay the mortgage and deposit one hundred bulls into the account. Can my fiancée access it?

"Yes, it's a joint account." I thanked the clerk and walked back home to have lunch with Carolena. I walked through the door of the bakery and saw Carolena exchanging bread and some other baked goods with a customer. The customer walked up to me and said,

"Oh, you must be Allen. So nice to have a godly man living here now instead of those freaks." I nodded and the customer walked out of the bakery as I went to Carolena and asked,

"Who was that? How did she know my name?"

"Oh, that was Michelle, the butcher's wife, but more importantly, you're late, Allen. Where were you?"

"I got paid today, so I went to the bank to make a deposit. I also paid the mortgage."

"Ah, well, I was going to use the money I've made over the past week to do that. I can keep some now to get groceries, so thank you, Allen!" She said and kissed me on the cheek.

"Oh, and talking about money, I got you this." Carolena handed me a piece of leather that could be unfolded to reveal a large pouch that could be used for storing money. I learned it was called a wallet. I thanked Carolena as I took the money I had out of the envelope and placed it inside the wallet.

As we ate the lunch Carolena had warmed on the stove, I could not shake the banishment of those homosexuals from my mind. I had embraced and trusted God and Carolena told me that the Bible clearly defined homosexuality as an abomination, but in the Bible, Jesus Christ said that only those without sin can cast the first stone. I don't think the Tyrians were justified in taking God's judgment upon themselves. I decided to keep these thoughts to myself. It felt safer to do so, as it did with turning 9900M into Jason instead of letting him reveal Consciousness Decay to the Androids. If I had to keep secrets in human society just as I did in the AEF, was humanity truly better than the Androids? That was a thought

I could not shake regardless of how much I focused on my work.

Despite the thoughts running through my mind, my work for the week went well. The bunker had the ability to manufacture electronics and a small amount of raw materials to do so. I had made lengths of various thicknesses of wire, a circuit breaker box, and a light bulb. I began my work on electrifying Tyre by laying a thick high-voltage cable underground, and I had laid enough to reach the bakery by the end of Saturday.

After Sunday mass, Mary had me try on the tuxedo she made for my wedding. It fit me well, and even though I did not have a great understanding of the aesthetics of clothing, I could tell it was a special outfit. Mary said she would keep my tuxedo in the shop until it was time for the wedding, which was to be held in three weeks at the church. When I arrived at home, I found Carolena waiting for me.

"Did the tux fit ok?" she asked.

"It did, so I'm ready for our wedding."

"Well, that's a relief! Wedding dresses are something else. Anna told me they'll all have to work on it to get it done a few days before the wedding." Carolena rubbed the ring finger on her left hand, staring at me, and said. "W-We need to get rings too. Can you go to the jeweler and give them our ring sizes? Mine's four and a half and they can measure your size there." I nodded and Carolena blushed and looked away for a moment before saying, "C-Can you get an engagement ring for me too? A man usually gives an engagement ring to a woman to show his love for her and to propose marriage. I've always wanted one since I was a little girl, but I proposed to you so..." Carolena looked around the room timidly and tapped her index fingers together. I grabbed her ring finger and smiled.

"So that's why it's the ring finger. I'll get you an engagement ring since I do love you." I kissed Carolena. This was the first time I kissed her myself. It felt natural, loving, and human to kiss a woman that I loved.

Chapter 15

After I was done with my guard work for the day, I headed to the jeweler's, which was the nicest building I had visited in Tyre so far. The exterior was built entirely out of marble and the interior was marble as well, which was cut and shined to be flawless. The room was draped in fine satin clothes, which had display cases full of jewelry made of gold, silver, and various gemstones. A man wearing an outfit similar to a tuxedo greeted me,

"Hello, Sir. How may I help you today?"

"My name is Allen Katona. I'm getting married soon and I need to give this establishment mine and my fiancée's ring sizes. I also need an engagement ring."

"Ah, yes! The Katona wedding. We've been wondering when we'd see one of you two. I can measure your size and if you have your fiancée's, we can get started on the rings today."

"Thank you. Carolena, my fiancée's ring size is four and a half." I extended my hand and the jeweler put several metal rings over my finger before settling on one and saying,

"Size thirteen. You're quite the man, Allen. Well, now that's done, let's talk engagement rings for your lucky lady." He pulled out a case, opened it, and laid it on the table. It contained engagement rings. I grabbed the one that caught my eye first. The band was golden with a small white gemstone that shone in the most beautiful way.

"Ah! Great eye. That's my best one and it's yours for five thousand bulls." After the jeweler told me the price, I set the ring down. It was the ring I felt I needed to express my love for Carolena with. I quickly deduced that I could use the PTM to make a replica and told the jeweler that I had to leave for lunch.

Machine to Man

Before I headed to the bakery for lunch, I went to the bunker where I had stored my PTM, which I had used to manufacture the electronics for Tyre. I repurposed a small amount of unused nanosteel and made a replica of the ring. The band was quite large, but it would resize once Carolena wore it. I put it in my pocket and I headed home along with the PTM. I opened the door and saw Carolena, who had just finished setting the table for lunch. She smiled when she saw me, and greeted me by saying,

"Perfect timing. It got busy, so I got a late start to making lunch." I walked towards Carolena, grabbed her left hand and put the engagement ring I made onto her ring finger and kissed her. She pulled away after a moment to admire the ring, saying,

"Oh, Allen, how did you get a ring like this? It's divine!"

"I saw it at the jeweler's, but it was too expensive, so I made a replica." Carolena's eyes teared up, as she grabbed my hands and said,

"It is really nice, but it means so much more knowing that you made it!" She kissed me on the cheek and dried her eyes as she ushered me to sit down and eat lunch with her. After we finished our meal, I began my work on electrifying our home. Our home had a small yard in the back. It was surrounded by an aged fence that barely blocked the road and the next row of houses behind it from sight. I used the PTM to dig a hole near the house and to run the wire from the generator to a circuit breaker box I installed on the back wall covered by an awning. I then ran three circuits. One for each story. I installed lighting fixtures on the ceiling of each story of the house and light switches to control them. When I finally finished this work, night had fallen. Carolena was about to light a candle when I used the light switch to turn on the light bulbs to illuminate the room. Carolena dropped the candle and match she was holding and exclaimed,

"Oh, wow! It's like daytime! How's this possible?"

63

"It's electricity. The light bulbs I've installed use the flow of electrons to create friction, which produces light and heat."

"Electrons? Electricity? You were talking about stuff like that, but it led to something amazing like this. Is making light the only thing you can do with this electricity of yours?"

"No, I also made radiators that can heat a room more effectively than a fireplace, and there were countless machines humans used to make that ran off of electricity."

"Can you make those machines?"

"Not exactly. I have no specific schematics and the bunker has no electronics other than what's necessary to make it survivable for humans."

"Well, you're a genius, Allen. This is amazing! It's like nothing I've ever seen before, and if anybody can figure out more ways to use electricity, it's you, Allen."

"Thank you for the praise." I grabbed my stomach as it growled.

"Well, of course, you'd be hungry!" Carolena giggled "Usually, it'd be hard to cook this late, but with your light bulbs, it'll be a cinch!" Carolena vaulted downstairs and into the kitchen. She found the light switch and flipped it, which illuminated the kitchen. She looked at the kitchen in amazement and began to cook dinner. I was in the kitchen with her and helped her prepare the meal. It was my first time cooking, and as such, I wasn't much help. But regardless, Carolena appreciated my efforts. The day ended for us soon after we finished our dinner.

Over the next three weeks, I taught Samson's sons, Harry and Michael, the process of wiring buildings and installing lights as well. This allowed me to install circuit breaker boxes on several houses in a day while Harry and Michael would do the rest of the work for each building. With this division of labor, we had wired every house in the North District with willing owners the day before the wedding.

Chapter 16

Our wedding was on Sunday in the church in lieu of Sunday mass. Carolena had woken up and left for Smith's home. I turned on the lights and saw a simple breakfast and a note placed on the nightstand. The note read: "I love you, Allen. Hope this sets you up for our special day." Below the written text was an imprint of Carolina's lips. She had told me of cosmetics used to enhance beauty, including lipstick, which she used to create the imprint on the note. After reading it, I folded it and stashed it in my wallet. I then ate my breakfast, got dressed in my tuxedo, and headed to the church. I opened the door to the church and Samson greeted me.

"Ah! The man of the hour! We've got some time before the ceremony starts, so let's chat outside for a couple of minutes." We went outside and we leaned against the stone wall of the church. Samson pulled out a small wooden box and slid the cover off, pulling out two cylindrical articles that Samson called cigars. He lit both with a match and showed me how to smoke it, before handing one to me. We smoked as we chatted.

"They don't let the farmers grow too much tobacco these days, so these are for special occasions only, like today. You like it, Al?"

"There is a flavor. It's different from eating and drinking, but I like it."

"Glad you like it, Al. Caro's almost ready, but we've still got some time."

"Ok. Well, Carolena told me what to do, but I still feel nervous."

"That's normal, Al. Marriage is a lifelong commitment. Just stay calm, stand by her, and you'll both be fine," Samson said, as he patted my shoulder. "I'll help you out too, Al. You never had a father and Caro lost hers, so I'm the best you got."

"Thank you, Samson. Carolena told me how important a father is in a wedding, so it means a lot to her that you're filling the void as best you can." Samson puffed on his cigar and said, "Yeah, what happened was tragic, but on the bright side, at least you don't have to meet your in-laws!"

"Sam! That's terrible to say even as a joke!" Mary ended our conversation and ushered Samson to the back of the church and told me to make my way to the altar. In a matter of minutes, the ceremony started with Penelope walking between the pews and throwing flower petals haphazardly around herself. Mary was sitting in one of the pews closest to me and grabbed Penelope and sat her on her lap. Next were Anna and Caitlin, who were wearing the same satin red dress and were each with a man whom I did not know. The four of them made their way to the front pews and sat down. Finally, Carolena and Samson walked down the aisle. She looked beautiful. Once she came into my sight, the only thing I could look at was her. Her dress was pure white and had lace woven throughout it. A transparent piece of fabric called a veil was covering her face and her hair was braided with daisies placed throughout the braids. Samson released his grip on Carolena and sat next to Mary as Carolena approached me. I lifted the veil over her head as Carolena had instructed me to do so before the ceremony began and a priest that was standing between us began to speak:
"Dearly beloved children of God. We are gathered here today to join two young souls in the holy bonds of marriage..." I was holding Carolena's hands and looking deeply into her eyes. We vowed to love each other until the end of our days, in sickness and in health. We put golden wedding rings on each other's ring fingers, then kissed to conclude the ceremony. There was great music, and the connection I had with Carolena made it the most pleasurable experience I've had as a human so far.

After the ceremony was over, a lively party called a reception was held in the basement of the church. We spent the night eating, drinking, and conversing with everyone there. It was late into the night when the reception ended and we made our way home.

Machine to Man

After the wedding was the honeymoon. Carolena told me little of what we'd do during our honeymoon other than the fact that it would involve only us. Carolena unlocked the door and we made our way to our bedroom. I sat on the bed while Carolena went into the bathroom. A few minutes passed, and Carolena emerged and sat on the bed. She was wearing only underwear and a transparent piece of fabric that clasped at the back and parted at her midriff. She grabbed my hand and placed it on her cheek. I pulled her towards me and kissed her. She panted as she began to undress me, saying, "Al-Allen, now we're going to make love."

Chapter 17

Our honeymoon lasted a week and we spent most of the time engaging in the act of sexual intercourse with each other. Carolena insisted that I only refer to it as making love in her presence. Regardless of the name, it was the most pleasurable thing I had felt as a human so far, and I was disappointed when our honeymoon ended and we didn't have the same amount of time to set aside to make love.

I came back home from my first guard shift after the honeymoon and saw Carolena standing in front of the counter. She ran up, embraced, and kissed me, circling her finger on my chest and whispering into my ear, "Lunch will be done in about half an hour, so we've got some time to fool around." I smiled, and Carolena was about to lock the door when Lily burst in and said,

"Just because you got hitched to my Allie doesn't mean you get him all to yourself."

"Yes it does!" Carolena pushed Lily away from me and slapped her. "Allen told me that you groped him! You disgusting harlot!"

"Yeah, and it was better for him than whatever you can do!" Lily was about to slap Carolena back, but I grabbed her hand before she could and said,

"You're not welcome here, Lily! Leave us alone!" Lily's face turned red, and I could feel her legs tremble as she leaned more of her weight onto me.

"Oh, Allie, I know you'd love to do it rough. You're such a beast!" I let go of her hand and backed away as she continued to speak.

"Well, I'm actually here on official business. Some friends of mine need gold, and we've got word that that Android city has a whole stockpile, and who better to help me steal some than you, Allie!

You were an Android for a century, right? You must know that place like the back of your hand!"

"The AEF does stockpile gold for electronics manufacturing, but why would I help you? Why would I leave my wife to get gold for your friends?"

"Because you have to! Go talk to Maury and he'll vouch for me." I stormed out and made my way to Maury's office. I walked so quickly that I was practically running, and I stormed into Maury's office and said: "I just got married and you're telling me to go back to the AEF with that woman?!?"

"Calm down, Allen! Sit down and I'll explain." I clenched my fist and inhaled and sat down in front of Maury's desk. Maury spoke:

"That's a good man, Allen. I'm assuming Lily came by and gave you the gist of what you two will be doing. The Central Bank of Tyre needs more gold. We don't have enough to back up all the paper notes. If people can't exchange bulls for gold, the whole economy collapses. It happened when my grandfather was mayor. The riots lasted for weeks. Allen, when we first met, I told you that you'd have to serve Tyre to earn my trust. Now's the time to do so, Allen. I know you're a newlywed, but your city needs you to do this. Your family will have nothing but ash if you don't get the gold the bank needs, so please go."

"I suppose I couldn't go alone."

"No, I owe Lily some... well, a lot of favors, so that's non-negotiable." I sighed and shook Maury's hand and walked back slowly to prepare for what I had to do next.

Chapter 18

It took two days to prepare for our journey. I was at the north gate with Carolena, Lily, and Samson. Samson shook my hand and patted my shoulder.

"Don't worry 'bout a thing here, Al. Me and the girls'll make sure Caro's right as rain."

"Thanks, Samson." Carolena hugged and kissed me. "Come back soon and safe, Allen, and don't let that harlot seduce you! You have to be godly, not worldly."

"I promise." I kissed Carolena and saw Lily roll her eyes. I broke away from Carolena and began walking so quickly towards the AEF that Lily had to run to catch up to me and said:

"Hey! Slow down! It's really early, so I'm too tired to walk this fast."

"The faster we walk, the sooner this will be over. If you're too tired, then stay behind; that's fine with me." Lily frowned and kept walking. We walked from morning until the sun began to set. We set up a camp, ate, and slept. I didn't let her talk to or come near me. This was our routine for eight days until we arrived at the facility where I made my human body. Lily looked up at the large gray monolith of a building and said,

"This isn't a city, Allie. Why are we here?"

"Only an Android can infiltrate the AEF, so we've got to make one."

"How are we going to do that?"

"I'm going to put your mind in my old body, then I'll figure out what to do next." Lily bit her lip and moaned.

"Well, I wanted you to be inside of me, but I'll take this for sure!" I sighed and opened the door. We both grabbed our ears as it screeched open, then we made our way inside. Lily walked around the facility, staring at everything she could with intent curiosity while I went to the armory to retrieve my body and lay it on a table next to an empty pod. Lily walked up to me and laid a hand on my body that was lying on the table.

"I can't believe you were in this thing and now I'm going to be too! How do we even do that?"

"You're going to get in that pod and I'll be able to transfer your consciousness from there. Your body will be suspended in fluid and I'll put an oxygen mask on you so you can switch back to an alive body." Lily giggled, and she stripped naked.

"Well, I don't want to get my clothes wet and you do deserve a show like what you see?"

"I don't want to be with you, Lily. Get in the pod so we can get this over with." Lily sighed as she climbed into the pod. I grabbed an oxygen mask that was attached to the inside of the pod and helped her put it on her face. I closed the pod and began filling it with fluid to begin the process of transferring Lily's mind to my Android body.

Chapter 19

To accurately describe the events that occurred after Lily assumed control of my former body, I transcribed her experiences below:

After Allie closed the pod, I instantly fell asleep, then I woke up moments later. I shot up and saw the tube that was containing me. It felt so weird to see my body and even weirder to see my hands and my whole body as metal. I tried to scream, but I heard no sound. I heard Allen say,

"Ok, I can use my computer to communicate with you now."

"Why can't I talk?"

"You have no vocal cords, so you can't produce audible sound as you can in your human form. Androids transmit their thoughts to each other through radio waves, and I'm using my computer to intercept and transcribe the thoughts you are transmitting."

"Ok, that makes some sort of sense, so what's next? What's the plan, Allie?"

"One kilometer away from the AEF is a vehicle. We'll head there then I'll help you slip into one of the patrols around the AEF and guide you to the factory where the gold is stored and you can transport it out from there."

"Ok well then let's begin. The sooner I'm done with being a machine, the better." We got up and made our way to the Android city.

It took a few hours to get to the vehicle Allie was talking about. He said it still worked even after spending decades in the forest. He used his devices to connect to the Android city and make it seem like I belonged in one of the patrols. He also uploaded a map and more information into my head. The whole experience was odd, but I was able to wrap my head around it. Allen made a metal backpack and placed it on me. He told me that along with gold, some amount of nanosteel was in the same stockpile. The backpack would automatically absorb the nanosteel and, in turn, allow us to steal more gold. Allen told me that once I entered the city, I'd have an hour to get this done before I was automatically deleted from the system and the security measures for the factory that he disabled would be reengaged. He disconnected from the city and told me to go. My vision showed arrows directing me to the closest patrol, so I ran quickly and, soon, I was at the patrol.

"Identify yourself to us and state your purpose," said one of the Androids.

"I am unit 6900S. I completed all necessary patrols for the day and have business in the AEF."

"Affirmative. You may follow us." Relief washed over me as I followed them and made my way into the Android city. I saw a timer start in the corner of my vision and the words "clearout protocol engaged" flash. A massive group of Androids left so a maintenance worker, who was already stationed there by Allie, could do a routine inspection but ignore me. This left me free to enter the factory and walk out with the gold unseen. His abilities amazed me. The worker would even report that it was only there for the exact time that I was. The stockroom was as boring as everything else these machines built and had a lot of things I could not recognize at all, but in the center on metal platforms were piles of neatly stacked gold bars. The backpack identified them and began to automatically store them as I walked towards them. The backpack was able to find enough nanosteel to steal all the gold the city had on hand, which amounted to two tons. I snuck out of the factory and ran towards a maintenance exit on the wall of the city to leave and get back to Allie. I ran away from the Android city and was able to get back to him quickly and place the backpack on the ground. Allie was sleeping on top of the vehicle. I shook him awake and said: "I got the gold, Allie, let's go." He smiled and broke down the backpack and used the nanosteel to store the gold on the vehicle and make it able to carry all the weight and still move. We drove the vehicle to the facility, and Allen parked it right by the entrance, and we quickly went inside. I lay down on the table next to my human body, and Allen put me back where I belonged.

Chapter 20

Lily got on the table, and I transferred her mind back into her body. She would be asleep for about an hour, which gave me time to store my body back in the armory and eat a meal. When I finished, I saw that Lily had emerged, dried and clothed herself.

"God, I'm tired, Allie! Can we go home now?"

"Yes, we're done, and I want to see Carolena so badly."

"UGH! I was just naked in front of you and you're still thinking of her! You're just as much of a square as she is!"

"I love her, she's done a lot for me and I won't betray her no matter what! Can you please respect that?"

"Whatever. I'm too tired to argue. Let's just go." We left after that conversation and made our way into the vehicle. The journey back was much quicker with the vehicle. We only made one stop so we could relieve ourselves, and before I got back into the vehicle, I smelt corpses. I spent too much time around them to forget the smell. I walked in the direction of the smell, and Lily followed me. We found two corpses; they were both holding hands and each had a knife in their other hand. They were both wearing necklaces, which caught Lily's eye, and she exclaimed,

"It's Billy and Johnny! The two boys you saw getting banished when you first got here. They made those necklaces for each other, like wedding rings. Oh, they were so cute together!"

"You knew them?"

"Yeah, I'd watch them go at each other all the time and sometimes they'd even get me off too! Also, they were both great bakers. Everyone loved their bread and treats, including me, so who cares if they fucked each other's asses? This was too cruel on them. I figured they'd do this; they weren't up to it to survive outside of Tyre."

"Well, you're disgusting, but I'll bury them. I know they sinned, but through Jesus' sacrifice, they may be able to find peace. I'll pray for it."

"You're so smart, Allie. Why believe all that nonsense?"

"I have faith and you should too. It's a wonderful thing to believe in something greater than yourself." Lily sighed, and I went ahead to bury Billy and Johnny. After a few minutes, we made our way back to Tyre. We were able to get to the north gate just before the sun was about to set. Samson saw us on top and in ten minutes. Maury emerged with a large metal cart being drawn by four horses. A group of us, along with Maury, loaded the gold rather quickly. Just before they were about to leave, Maury said,

"I can't believe you did it, Allen, and it's only been nine days. I'm sure you too are tired. I'll let you get some rest now, but we'll talk longer and in much greater detail soon." Maury then got on the cart and left. I saw Carolena run up from behind the cart to hug and kiss me deeply. I saw tears run down her cheek as she said:

"Oh, thank the Lord you're safe!"

"Yes, and hopefully I won't have to leave again or be around her."

"So rude, Allie!" Lily sighed. "But I guess I did push your buttons a little too much. You're still pretty innocent." She giggled as Carolena kissed and hugged me again and asked, "So nothing happened between you two?"

"No, your man is just as plain as you, unfortunately."

"Oh, thank God! Now I feel great about telling you this! Allen, I think I'm pregnant!"

Part Three: Our Family

Our family, they can't be a mistake!

Chapter 21

U GH! So not fair! Why can't you put a bun in my oven?"

"I'm the only one who can have his babies, harlot! You're not godly enough to be a mother, but I am, and so the Lord blessed us both!"

"You said "think", which means you don't know for certain." Carolena placed my hand on her stomach, and the thought of Carolena and I having a family again made me smile. I wanted her to be happy so I needed to be sure.

"Well, I missed my period two days ago, my chest feels really tender and I've got morning sickness really bad."

"Morning sickness? But it's nighttime."

"No, silly, it just means I'm nauseous all the time."

"Ok, well if I got a sample of your blood or urine, I could test it to see if it contains human chorionic gonadotropin."

"Human what now?"

"Human chorionic gonadotropin is a hormone secreted by the embryo to prepare your body for pregnancy. If it's being produced in your body, it would be in your urine or blood."

"I've got no idea what you're saying, but it sounds like we'd really know for sure if you could use science to test for a pregnancy. It's a little weird, but I can pee in a cup for you." Carolena and I laughed, and we kissed. We hadn't noticed that Lily had left until now. We went back home, and I only bathed and then fell asleep holding Carolena tightly.

The next day came, and Maury came knocking on our door early in the morning. He invited and ushered me into his office, eager to talk to me, but only after having breakfast with Carolena and me. He started the conversation by saying,

"The gold is in the vault. We've got enough to last decades even when we start printing bulls again. So great job on that one. I talked to Lily and she said you connected to that Android city so you two could easily steal the gold. Did you learn anything?"

"Yes, the AEF is manufacturing atom-ripping bombs. They're bombs that essentially turn all matter in its small radius into dirt."

"How small?"

"A single bomb could destroy Tyre, but it wouldn't touch the surrounding forest."

"Jesus! they probably want to bomb Tyre. Do they know you're here?"

"No, my disappearance was documented and they did search for me but were unable to track where I went. I was able to cover my tracks by initially leaving, but this theft might have revealed me. I'm certain they will deduce that I stole the gold, whether I was able to cover my tracks well enough or not."

"Sounds about right. We should prepare for these atom-ripping bombs. Please tell me there's a way."

"Yes, the bunker below Tyre is made of nanosteel, which can't be destroyed by atom-ripping bombs since they're also made of nanosteel.

"Well, that's great news. Our population is about one million. Can you fit all of us in that bunker?"

"Not in its current state it was designed to house five hundred thousand but I should be able to modify it within a few years. The Androids require gold to manufacture the bombs, so their plans are most likely set back. I think we have plenty of time."

"Well, that's a relief, but I'm not taking any chances with this many lives on the line. You'll only work guard shifts every other week. Use the extra time to get the bunker ready as soon as you can. From now on, I'll pay you ten thousand bulls per month on salary. You've earned it! Of course, you'll still have to tithe and pay your taxes like a good citizen!" I shook his hand. "Thank you, Maury. I'm pretty sure Carolena's pregnant, so this will make things easier for us."

"Well, congratulations, and I'm happy to help. I'll tell Hariti, and she'll see your wife through this. She's the best midwife in Tyre." I nodded, thanked Maury, and left to go back home, where I saw Carolena running the bakery. It was filled with customers that were intoxicated by the happiness and glow that she had filled her bakery. I sat down and rested my eyes as Carolena did her work. About thirty minutes passed before I heard her sit down and say,

"I'm closing up the shop early today so we can spend some time together. I just wanted to make sure the grocers had enough bread for the day."

"Thank you. I've really missed you."

"What did you talk with Maury about? You were away for a while."

"I think the Androids are planning to attack Tyre. I'm going to make sure everyone in the city is safe, and Maury will be paying me ten thousand a month to do so."

"Oh, wow! Do we really need that much money, though? But more importantly, this attack, how soon do you think it is?"

"Most likely years, since they started after I left, and the gold we stole will set them back considerably."

"Well then, let's not worry about the future and focus on the present. Allen, I really do think I'm pregnant, but I did go pee in a cup and it's in our bathroom. Whatever you were talking about yesterday, you can do now."

"Ok then, I will. It should only be a few minutes." I went upstairs and entered the master bathroom of our home and saw a cup with a small amount of urine in it. I grabbed the PTM from our bedroom and used it to make a test strip that would transmit its results to my computer. I submerged the test strip and waited for the results as Carolena came upstairs. The test was finished. The levels of human chorionic gonadotropin in her urine indicated that she was indeed pregnant. I cleaned the test strip, integrated it into the PTM, and disposed of the urine as Carolena came into the bathroom.

"Well, am I pregnant?" I walked up to Carolena and I kissed her.

"I can confirm that you are." She cried out in joy and hugged me as we kissed. We walked into the bedroom and fell onto the bed, making love for so many hours. I had missed her dearly, and I was so glad to be able to feel her love again. After we had gotten enough of each other. We bathed, had a simple dinner, and went to bed for the night.

Chapter 22

I yawned as I stood in the watchtower next to Samson. Being paid on salary meant that I didn't have to clock in for my shifts at the tower, but I still had to show up on time and report to Bill. I stretched and tried to stay awake.

"You two were practically up all day and night going at it. The whole district practically heard you two. Makes sense you're tired," said Samson.

"Well, I missed her, and it's very fun to make love."

"Amen to that brother, but get it while you can. You two won't have much time for it once the kid comes."

"How'd you know Carolena was pregnant?"

"She was so sick a few days ago that Anna and Caitlin had to open up shop for her, so we figured you had knocked her up."

"Well, I'm certain I know how to test for it and she's definitely pregnant."

"Of course you'd have a way for that, and congratulations. I'm sure you'll be a great father, Al!"

"Thanks, Samson. It feels good to hear that from you." I was too tired to do much else, so our conversation for the day ended there and we stood in silence and stewed in boredom until lunchtime came. I arrived at the bakery to find Carolena sitting at one of the tables, talking with Hariti. I heard her say,

"I've been a midwife to dozens of mothers and I have eight of my own with Maury. I promise I'll do everything I can to make this pregnancy go off without a hitch!"

"Thanks Hariti, I really appreciate it. I-I always thought my mother would be here to help me through this. I wish she could see her grandchildren. My father too." Hariti hugged Carolena, and when she noticed me standing at the entrance, she said,

"Speaking of fathers, there's one. Come sit down, Allen. I just got here, so you didn't miss much." I sat down and I held Carolena's hand as Hariti explained that she would come once a week to see how Carolena's pregnancy was progressing and to help us prepare our home for the child that we would welcome into the world relatively soon. She got up and left after she bid us farewell and I ate lunch with Carolena. I was about to leave when Carolena grabbed my hand and said,

"I almost forgot! Our marriage certificate came the day after you left. You need to sign it, then I can finally frame it." She rushed upstairs and grabbed a thick white piece of paper that read:

Certificate of Marriage

This certifies that Carolena Katona née Barstow, born May 22 2181, and Allen Katona, born May 23, 2177

were married on June 29, 2200 in the North Tyre Church in a holy union recognized under Tyrian law.

Underneath this text were two spaces to sign, one with Carolena's signature. I signed my name on the other space and Carolena smiled and said, "It's official! I am now Mrs. Katona!" She kissed me on the cheek, and I continued on with the rest of the day. I had just left the bakery when a man approached me. Even from a distance, I could tell that he was angry. This man was the oldest human I had met so far. I was aware of how humans deteriorate with age, but to see it as a human right in front of me was nothing like knowing it from deadpan medical descriptions. The man pointed his finger at me and stretched his neck upwards to make eye contact, saying,

"I'm the chandler for the north district and you've practically ruined me!"

"Chandler? What do you mean?"

"I'm Alec Chandler. My family has made candles here since Tyre was first built a century ago!"

"I suppose light bulbs do eliminate the need for candles in most cases."

"Yes! We've only got one tenth of the customers now. I don't know what to do if this keeps going on like this. You're the one who did this! Who made so many brazenly take up this new way of lighting homes! You need to make this right!"

"I will. I can show you how to make light bulbs. The ones I've installed will break soon and people will need replacements. I'll let you manufacture them so you can sell them instead of candles."

"Bah! I'm too old to learn new tricks. My children and grandchildren will probably be able to. Come tomorrow afternoon and you can show them." I nodded and we went our separate ways. I headed to the bunker and began to plan its expansion. The bunker consisted of a main entrance that led to a living area that could house five hundred thousand, which was connected to a large swath of artificial farmland, and a control room, which was connected to the workshop and generator that I had utilized prior. This was all housed under a thick layer of nanosteel. There was enough room below the earth to build an additional living area and artificial farmland to support it and still leave room for additional sections if necessary. It was dinnertime when I had finished this planning and the preparation to gather materials to build the first living area, which I would start tomorrow. I made my way home and had dinner with Carolena, then we went to sleep for the night.

Machine to Man

The morning came and passed by uneventfully. I had a quick lunch with Carolena, and then I made my way to the Chandler residence and knocked on their door. A young woman who looked like she was Carolena's age opened the door and said:

"Oh! You must be the man Grandpa was talking about." We just finished lunch, so you're right on time. Come on in!"

"That's good to hear. I'm Allen, by the way." I walked into the home as she told me her name was Alice. I followed her to a workshop. It was filled with candles and equipment to make large amounts of them. Towards the back, there was a large table with nothing on it. I set down the PTM and the raw materials to make light bulbs. I set up the PTM to make a machine that would turn sand and metal ore into the glass, filament, and wiring needed to make a light bulb and another to shape those materials into the completed bulbs. Alice was very receptive to the process, and it took less than a week of lessons for her to master the process of making light bulbs. I was able to resume work on the bunk unhindered just as my first week free of security shifts started. I had decided against going forward with electrifying more of Tyre until the bunker was done and I could determine how to keep Tyre's businesses from being ruined by replacing them with electrical appliances.

Chapter 23

The first day of the new week started quite peacefully as Carolena let me sleep in about an hour later than I normally would. I stumbled downstairs and Carolena already had breakfast ready. I tried to eat quickly, but Carolena insisted I slow down by saying:

"Honey! I put a lot of love into every meal. I want you to taste it!"

"I-I know, but I've a lot to do. I can't let what happened to you happen again. I..." Carolena kissed me and held my hand. "Didn't you say that we had a lot of time? Relax, take time to do things right, and make time for your wife, especially when she's pregnant!" I nodded and slowed down, and we had a lovely conversation before I headed out and went to the bunker to continue my work. I was able to automate the material gathering process that needed to happen before I could begin work on the expansion of the living and farming areas of the bunker. The bunker had enough construction materials on hand that were stored in the workshop for me to begin work on a small armory next to the main entrance. By spending as much time and energy as I could building the armory, I was able to finish by Saturday evening. On Sunday morning, during church, all I could think was that I had a new, perfectly built armory that had no weapons or supplies and was therefore useless. I told Carolena of my predicament as we ate lunch after church, and she said,

"Didn't that facility where you made your human body have weapons?"

"Yeah! So much has happened that I forgot. I'm still getting used to that."

"Androids don't forget things, do they?"

"No, and I still remember every second of my life as an Android and everything I learned during that time. It's very useful and it's helped us a lot, but it haunts me." Carolena held my hand tightly and encouraged me to go. I could make the round trip in a day if I used the vehicle and traveled quickly. I did so, and the sun had just begun to set as I arrived at the facility. I used the PTM to gather the useful supplies that the armory had, which were two thousand pairs Standard Issue Assault Rifles and Standard Issue Pistols, one ton of ammunition, and five hundred pounds of MREs. I was surprised to see that my body was still there. It made me hopeful that I had successfully eluded the AEF. I cleared my mind and I drove the vehicle as quickly as I could and was able to get back to Tyre just as the sun was about to rise. It didn't take long for me to stow the supplies in the armory I had built. I stumbled to the watchtower and tried to check in for my shift. Bill stopped me by saying, "You're late anyway, and you look like shit. Go home and get some sleep." I thanked Bill and I stumbled off home and into bed.

Chapter 24

I slept until the next morning, and stumbled out of bed in a haze. I spent the morning recovering from the supply run I did. Lunchtime came, and Harry and Michael came to eat lunch with us.

"It's been a while, but it's nice to see you, Al. Mind if Mikey and me eat lunch with you two?" Harry asked as Carolena set two more plates, saying,

"You boys are lucky; I made a lot for lunch, but try to give me some notice next time."

"Sorry, Caro. This was kind of spur of the moment. The harvest is winding down, so Mikey and I are going to have more time on our hands..." Michael interjected by saying,

"Yeah, and that means we can wire up more homes. We already did the North district, but the South, West, East, and Central districts still haven't, and people have been begging us to wire up their homes. We need your help, Al!"

"Yeah, we can wire the homes by ourselves, but we can't connect them to the generator and we don't have much in terms of materials." Harry said

"Well, I don't have much in terms of time, so I can't help like I did before. I can make a device that can wire homes to the mainframe, and I can show you how to make the wiring and the breaker boxes. You can get light bulbs from the Chandlers."

"I heard that Alice learned how to make light bulbs from you," said Michael.

"Sounds good to me. Can we get started after we eat?" Harry said. I agreed as Carolena brought out lunch. We ate, and then we got to work. I showed Michael how to manufacture breaker boxes and wiring. I then made a simplified PTM that could only interact with the bunker's electrical grid and trained Harry how to use it. When both of them had learned how to do their respective roles, it was dinnertime. We walked back from the bunker, and we ran into Samson on the way back to our street.

"Did you show the boys how to wire buildings on their own, Al?" he asked.

"Sure did, and they really took to it. They're good kids."

"Hey, I'm sixteen, and Mikey's fourteen. We're not kids anymore; we're men."

"We sure are! We're going to wire homes on our own." Samson laughed and patted them on the shoulder.

"You both still got a long way to go to be men, but this is a step. Come on, all the girls are waiting for us to have dinner. Al, that includes your lovely wife!" I nodded and followed them into their home, where, sure enough, the rest of Samson's family and Carolena were waiting for us. We sat down and began to eat after Carolena said grace. As we ate, Anna talked to Harry and Michael.

"So can you boys wire homes on your own now?"

"Yeah, we spent the day with Al, and Mikey and I took to it pretty quick."

"Good! Now you boys can actually do something useful when it's not harvest season," Caitlin said, and she laughed with Anna. Harry's face was red with anger as he said, "We help out around here. We know how to make clothes for the miners, and Mikey and I make sure they all get their clothes, not just the one you have a crush on!"

"I don't have a crush on James! We're just friends!" Anna said, burying her now flushed face in her hands.

"Friends who spend that much spare time making out by the mines? Come on Annie, you two will both be twenty-one next year, so you'll both have to settle down." Caitlin giggled as Anna collected herself and replied,

"I know, I know. We do love each other, and I think he wants to marry me as much as I do, but we like the way things are. I just want some more time with this family."

"I thought you had to be married at age eighteen?" I asked.

"No, that's only if you're a refugee. Citizens don't have to marry until they turn twenty-one, and that's what I'll do with Jamie. I promise you guys. Now can we drop this and have a nice meal with our guests?" Anna ended that conversation, and the rest of the meal was fun and peaceful. We finished eating, and as Mary got ready to put Penelope to bed, I heard her say,

"Mommy! Why did Caro eat so much?"

"She's eating for two, dear. That's why."

"But she doesn't have two mouths. How can she eat for two?"

"There's a baby in her belly."

Machine to Man

"How does a baby get in your belly, Mommy?"

"I'll tell you when you're older. Now enough chit-chat; it's time for bed." Mary shushed Penelope and brought her upstairs and insisted on it being bedtime, much to the protest of Penelope. Carolena and I bid the Smith family a good night and we made our way back home. Carolena wrapped herself around my arm and said,

"I didn't eat that much, did I?" I laughed and kissed Carolena.

"I don't think you should worry about what a four-year-old has to say about your eating habits."

"You know what, you're right! Thanks, honey!" She giggled and kissed me. We made our way to our bedroom and quickly went to sleep.

The next guard shift passed by uneventfully, and so did lunch. I was about to leave for the bunker when Carolena stopped me, kissed me on the cheek, and said,

"I almost forgot to tell you. Maury needs to talk to you after lunch, so right now." I nodded, and I made my way to Maury's office. I knocked on his door, and he told me it was unlocked. I sat down in front of Maury's desk, and he said,

"I was able to talk to Lily today. She was here for only a day after you two came back, so I never got to talk to her about her side of the heist until she came back yesterday."

"Where was she?"

"She took some of that gold and went trading. She comes from a family of traders, after all. There's quite a few villages to the south that have things we can only dream of, but that's beside the point. Lily told me that you turned her into an Android and you two were able to communicate without speaking and from a distance. Can you replicate that with two humans?

"I can create a device that transmits spoken words from one to another from a distance of five miles, but I'd advise against using such a device."

"Why's that? Is it harmful to humans?"

"No, radio waves are harmless to humans, but if we send messages over radio, the Androids can intercept them and be able to locate where they're sent from. They'd find Tyre, and, most likely, conclude that I am located here as well."

"I see. Not good a thing, but I can't help but think that we might need a device like that. There might be an emergency that justifies it."

"I don't know, Maury, but it's a simple device, a set of two, so two people can communicate with each other. I'll have it done before I have dinner."

"Thanks, Al. That's all I need for now. I'll see you when the devices are done." I left and headed to the bunker, where I went to the workshop and made the two radios in under an hour. I sat for a long time afterwards. I didn't feel comfortable giving these radios to Maury. I don't think anything would justify giving away Tyre's position to the Androids. I decided to give them to Maury despite my doubts. I was no leader, not in the AEF or in Tyre. I decided to play along with Maury as I had assumed that Androids were going to attack Tyre regardless of what I did. I gave the radios to Maury, and he locked them in a safe and prayed he never needed them. I nodded in agreement and went home. I had a fantastic night with Carolena, which took my mind off of the whole ordeal.

Chapter 25

The material gathering phase of the bunker's expansion ended, and I was able to work on it without any new disruptions. I noted the progress that Harry and Michael had made in wiring buildings. It took them two weeks to wire the entire Central district, which, unlike the North district, was willing to be wired. They made a considerable amount of money doing so and were able to buy the raw materials to make more wiring and breaker boxes and began to get to work on electrifying the Tyre's remaining three districts. Hariti committed to her promise to visit Carolena and didn't have much to report as she was early in the first of her three trimesters of pregnancy. Time went on and I worked as tirelessly as I could while I made time to spend with Carolena. Her pregnancy progressed well, and she slowly changed. Her stomach grew, which made her ankles swell and increased her need to urinate. Anna and Caitlin began helping Carolena run the bakery three months into her pregnancy. It was around this time that Harry and Michael had finished wiring all of the buildings in Tyre that were willing. The East and West districts were farmland, and most buildings didn't need electricity at all, and the rest were unwilling. The South district, however, was more dense and complicated than the North and Central districts, so they had to slow down to wire the buildings safely and, to add to that, the demand was high. Only ten buildings had unwilling owners. I was impressed with their accomplishments, and I was glad that electricity was beneficial to Tyre. I hoped to utilize electricity more once I had secured the city's safety. But to do that felt impossible to me, even though I had completed most of the expansion to the bunker and I had long ago managed to make a well stocked armory. I felt fear in the back of my mind no matter what. I tried to relax, and there were times when I could. It was near the end of Carolena's pregnancy, which was around nine months when I had completed the expansion. I told Maury, and he evaluated the facilities and was elated with the results. He left some time after me, and I sighed with relief. I had begun to feel safe as I left the bunker and right at the entrance was Lily, the smile on her face was off putting. She grabbed my hand and moaned as she said,

"Hey, Allie! You're finally done! I get to give you a present now!"

"W-What's that?"

"This." She placed one of the radios that I made for Maury in my hand. I snatched it in anger and asked,

"How'd you get this? I made it for Maury!"

"I talked the old fart into making them in the first place—or more like fucked him! I got the other one hidden five miles from here, so there's no chance of you disabling it, Allie. I know how big of a deal using one of these is too!"

"So why do this in the first place? Why threaten a whole city?"

"Because I love you, Allie, and with this, you'll have to notice me! I'll give you some more time to come to your senses, but you better leave her and come running for me or else the Androids will come running for you!"

"I can't leave Carolena. You might as well do it now!"

"Well, that wouldn't be any fun, and I think you'll see I'm the better woman soon enough. Oh, and don't think of telling that bitch about this or I will destroy this city." She kissed me on the cheek and ran off, wildly laughing all the while. I went back into the bunker and hid the radio. I could barely think. I breathed deeply and was able to collect myself. Lily sending the Androids to Tyre was a hypothetical. I had to focus and be there for what was actually happening. Carolena knew everything about my life. I felt immensely troubled that I could not confide in her. I left the bunker and went back home. I found

Carolena upstairs in a room we had dedicated for the baby, called a nursery. I had installed a crib a week ago, and she had just finished decorating the room when I arrived. I held her from behind and rested my hands on her stomach. She grabbed my hand and said,

"You're shaking, Allen. Why are you so nervous?"

"I'm scared, Carolena. Scared that I won't be able to do enough."

"Well, that's normal. This is our first time being parents and there's a lot to worry about with the Androids, but the bunker is finished, Allen. I know you and the Lord will keep us safe. I've prayed for it and it's come true before my eyes." I smiled and kissed Carolena.

"Thank you. I-I really needed to hear that. I love you."

"I love you too, Allen. Now tell me what you think of the nursery. I just finished it!"

"It's really nice. I think the baby will enjoy it here. I know I do." Carolena smiled, and we spent the rest of the night in each other's arms.

Chapter 26

A few days had passed since we finished the nursery, and I was making breakfast with her. I felt that she needed the help due to how pregnant she was, even though she insisted otherwise. We were almost ready to eat when Carolena collapsed onto the ground and cried out,

"ALLEN, THE BABY'S COMING! I'M GOING INTO LABOR!" I grabbed Carolena and brought her to our bedroom and laid her on the bed. I ran to the Smith house, burst through the door and said,

"CAROLENA IS IN LABOR. I NEED HELP!" Fortunately for me, Anna, Caitlin, Penelope, and Mary were downstairs. All four of them got up immediately, and Mary put a hand on my shoulder and said,

"Stay calm, Allen. We'll get Caro through this. Where is she?"

"She's in our bedroom."

"Perfect. We'll head over now and make sure she's ok. You go and get Hariti." I nodded and we all quickly left. In the corner of my eye, I could see them heading into the bakery as I ran towards Hariti's office. I desperately knocked on the locked door to her office the moment I arrived. After a few seconds, the door finally opened and Hariti appeared.

"Why are you banging on my door this early?" she asked.

"It's Carolena! She's in labor!" She darted back and grabbed a bag and told me to take her to Carolena, which I did. When we arrived, we saw Caitlin waiting with Penelope, who was trying to cover her ears from Carolena's screaming. We went upstairs and Hariti, along with Anna and Mary, helped her greatly through the labor process. I just held her hand and prayed for her health and safety and the same for the baby. It took fifteen hours of labor for her to give birth to a healthy baby boy. Hariti held the child and had me use a pair of scissors to cut his umbilical cord before wrapping the child tightly in a towel. We all sighed with relief, except Carolena, who gripped the bed sheets tightly and yelled,

"OH, GOD! I THINK ANOTHER ONE IS COMING!"

"You're right. You're having twins, Caro. Just keep pushing and breathing and this little one will come out much sooner." Hariti handed the crying baby to Anna, and fifteen minutes later, a baby girl was born. I cut the child's umbilical cord and Hariti wrapped the crying baby in a towel, and both of them were handed to Carolena. Hariti smiled at the sight of Carolena and tears welled up in her eyes.

"Let's leave these four alone for a while. I'll come back soon. It's difficult to breastfeed twins, so I can help you out if you're having trouble."

"Thank you all so much. I'm so happy. I feel so lucky to be a mother to two healthy children. I'll name them Jackson and Carolyn, after my parents."

"I think that's beautiful." I kissed Carolena on the cheek, and in that moment, I had never seen anything more lovely than the sight of Carolena holding our first two children. It was the beginning of our family. A family that was worth having, even with all the pain and anguish in our lives and the deaths of so many others. Becoming a human led to this, and I decided then and there that it was not a mistake for me to be human or for anyone to be. Like Hariti predicted, it was difficult for Carolena to breastfeed the children. I went downstairs and saw Samson, Mary, and Hariti having a conversation. Samson ran up to me when he saw me and patted me on the back, saying, "I heard the news that you had twins. That's twice the trouble for you two."

"Well, Carolena is happy, so I think it'll be worth it. Oh, you were right, Hariti. Carolena is having trouble breastfeeding, so she needs help."

"I'll get right to that then." Hariti walked off upstairs and I sat down. I hadn't slept or eaten the whole day, and the stress of Carolena's labor left me exhausted.

"You look like shit, Al. You should get some sleep. Mary and I will make sure Caro and the kids are alright, and I'll get Penny's old crib in the nursery too," Samson said, motioning for me to get up. I went into a free bedroom upstairs and slept off my exhaustion for as best and as long as I could as a young father.

Chapter 27

Carolena was far more experienced in child rearing than me, so it took me considerably more time to adjust to the constant crying, sleepless nights, and the experience of changing diapers that it entailed than for Carolena. I had two weeks off from work. The bakery was closed for this time as well. We bonded as a family, and it was a beautiful sight to see Carolena as a mother. The time went by quickly and she recovered from her labor. We also adjusted to life with two babies. The bakery reopened, and I went back to my guard shifts with Samson in the morning. When lunch time came, I saw Carolena feeding Jackson and Carolyn. Carolena smiled and said,

"These two need to eat so much! So lunch will be a little late. Well, it's a good thing Maury needs to talk to you." I kissed Carolena on the cheek and patted Jackson and Carolyn on their heads, and said goodbye as I made my way to Maury's office. This was the first time I would talk to Maury after I learned that he helped Lily blackmail me. I opened the door. My hands clenched into fists as Maury motioned for me to sit. I refused and said,

"I know what you did! You put a million lives at risk for what?!?"

"W-Well...I-I...You're right, Allen. It's just that I get bored with Hari, and that's even if she gives me any." I slammed my hands on the desk.

"A million lives! A whole city! Could all be nothing but dirt because you were bored? I'm disgusted."

"Well, when you put it like that, anyone would be. Look, I'm sorry, Al. I don't think anything will come of this. I'll find some way to bribe Lily, and she hasn't even been seen for months. I think we're in the clear."

"Ok. Well, is that the only thing you wanted to talk about?"

"No, I was talking to a miner about the bunker and he came up with an idea of making trenches that connect to the bunker."

"Trenches? Why?"

"So we can leave Tyre safely and defend ourselves from physical attacks if the Androids decide to do that before bombing us. I told him you were on board with the idea and that you two would meet tomorrow morning and start working on this project."

"I'll do this to keep my family and this city safe, not for you. I'll never trust you again."

"I wouldn't trust me either. I understand. And thank you, Allen. I nodded and walked off and spent the rest of the day with my family.

The next morning came and I made my way to the mines, which were about a mile away from the wall of the West district. A young man who was around my size shook my hand and greeted me.

"You're Allen, right? I'm James, James Ferris. I know you're pretty close with the Smith family. You might've heard of me since Annie's my girl.

"Yeah, I heard of you but not much and it was months ago too. Anna really does seem to love you, though."

"I do too. I just proposed to her. We're both turning twenty-one this year, so we gotta get hitched anyway. And when your twins came along, she got the baby fever real bad, man."

"Baby fever?"

"When girls see a baby, they want one too, or well, at least some of the time. Can't really tell what a woman's going to do till she does it." I thought of Lily and said,

"You can say that again." We both laughed and then planned the trench system. Three separate channels interconnected with a tunnel system that one would enter from the bunker's armory. We didn't know which direction the Androids would come from, so we had to encircle the entire city. This would be a massive project, and we decided to do it all manually so as to not raise suspicion in case the Androids were surveying the land surrounding Tyre, which they most likely were. We began our work the next day. I was able to use the bunker's technology and the PTM to build the tunnel system in a few weeks as James and his team of miners began work on the first trench. I came home from my first day of work digging the trenches exhausted and covered in dirt. I then took a shower and joined my family for dinner. As Carolena and I lay in bed that night, with my arms wrapped around her body, she said,

"I know we're really busy these days, but it's my birthday next week. It was also the day we first met and when my family died."

"Oh, I've lived for a hundred years and this one year has felt so much longer than all the rest."

"It's because you're human now, honey; you value your time. Anyway, I want it to be a happy day, so I'm inviting a bunch of people over for dinner. Also, I'd like a gift from you, Allen. I don't care what it is, as long as it's from the heart." I kissed her.

"I don't know anything about birthdays, but if it's important to you, then it's important to me." After talking for a while, we both fell asleep. I got up early the next morning and made my own breakfast, then I went to the jeweler. I was looking at a display that contained necklaces and one caught my eye. It was a thin gold chain that was tied to a golden, oval-shaped portrait of Mother Mary. A man approached me and said,

"That's one of our best ones. Would you like it?"

"Yes, it should be the perfect gift for my wife's birthday."

"I'll wrap it up for you then. You wouldn't happen to have five thousand bulls on you right now?"

"No. But I do have more than that in the bank, though."

"No problem then. I'll bring a bill of sale for you to sign, and the bank will take care of the rest." The man left and came back moments later. The necklace was in a long, thin box that was wrapped in brightly colored paper. I signed the bill of sale and headed back home. Carolena had just gotten up and was about to make breakfast, but she saw the gift and said,

"Oh, you got up early to get my gift. You're such a sweet guy!" I smiled and kissed Carolena and handed her the gift. She put it away in our bedroom quickly and then went downstairs to make breakfast. I got to work in the trenches early that day. Carolena's birthday arrived, and we had a party with Jamie and the Smith family at our house. We had a wonderful dinner and enjoyed a delicious and decorative cake. It was towards the end of the party when Carolena opened her gifts. She opened mine last and said,

"Oh, Allen, this is a beautiful necklace!" She put the necklace on, and it suited her perfectly. The party ended soon afterwards, and when Carolena and I were in bed, about to sleep for the night, she said to me,

"I know it's not a traditional birthday, but the day that you became human is in a few days and we should treat it like a birthday. Is there anything you want?"

"I just want to spend more time with you. That and making sure Jackson and Carolyn are safe." She kissed me good and smiled.

"You're a simple man, Allen. I love you." Three days later, my birthday came, and Carolena arranged for Mary to watch Jackson and Carolyn so she and I could have the night to ourselves. It was the first time we made love since the birth of our children, and it was wonderful and everything I could ever want as a gift.

Chapter 28

The work on the trenches progressed well. We had dug out all three trenches, but we still needed to reinforce them and connect them to my tunnel system. I was also installing weapon systems and laying traps and sensors. The next event of significance was the one-year anniversary of our wedding. Carolena told me it was a much more personal event that was meant to be celebrated only between us. We decided to not exchange gifts and just arranged to spend another night alone like we did on my birthday. Our anniversary was a workday, so I was working in the trenches when Hariti came to visit me and we had a private conversation.

"Allen, I just wanted to congratulate you on a successful year of marriage. You've both been very faithful to each other. I wish more marriages were like yours."

"You say that like you've known that Maury's betrayed you."

"I do. We lost our passion for each other a long time ago. but our marriage has to stay intact. There's nothing without family, Allen. That's why everyone has to be married and stay married."

"I don't think it's right to stand by men like Maury, but that's not a decision for me to make, I suppose." Our conversation ended there, and I finished my work for the day and came home to Carolena. We spent the rest of the day alone together and enjoyed another night of passion.

The trenches around Tyre took a total of eighteen months to complete. During that time, Carolynand Jackson grew considerably. They said their first words, which were "mama" and "flour", respectively. Anna and James also turned twenty-one during this time, but they were not allowed to have their wedding until after the trenches were finished. Most of the preparation for Anna and James' wedding was done, so the wedding was held a week after we finished the trenches built around Tyre and connected them to the tunnel system I had built. The wedding was very similar to ours, and it was joyous to see the start of a new family. I was still anxious about the impending conflict with the Androids and Lily, but I had prepared myself and Tyre as much as I could, and as such, this was the most relaxed I had felt as a human in a while.

I went back to work as a guard with Samson full time, which was as boring and uneventful as Samson described. It was around a week after the wedding when I was woken up by the sound of Carolena vomiting. She sat in bed next to me and patted her stomach and said to me,

"Allen, I know we've had more time to make love since Jack and Carrie have been able to sleep through the night for a while now, so I think I'm pregnant. Can you test me again?" I performed another pregnancy test and it came back positive, much to the joy of Carolena. We kissed and made love that night.

The news of Carolena's second pregnancy spread quickly, and I came home for lunch one day and found the bakery empty. I cautiously walked upstairs and saw the nursery door was open. I walked into it and saw Lily. She had Carolena pinned against a wall with a knife pointed at her chest. She turned her head to me and said,

"You dumbass, Allie! You knocked her up again! That's the opposite of what I wanted you to do!"

"Don't do this, Lily. You won't beat me in a fight. Let her go and we can figure something out! Please, I love her! I need her! Our children need her!"

"I can't live without you, and I know I can't beat you, but I know who can!" She grabbed Carolena and pushed her into my arms and pulled out the radio, activated it and said,

"I love you, Allie!" She grabbed the knife and slit her throat. She collapsed onto the ground and blood pooled around her body as the children woke up and began to cry.

Carolena grabbed Jackson and Carolyn and ran downstairs. I used the PTM to clean the nursery and carry Lily's corpse outside our home in a sanitary fashion. I stowed the radio on my person and then went outside and saw Maury, who recognized the corpse as Lily's and sighed as he said,

"Did you at least prevent her from using the radio?"

"No, she almost killed my wife then used it right before slitting her throat in front of my family."

"Jesus! Well, the morgue is close. At least bring her there, then get to the watchtower." We quickly made our way to the morgue. I went back home and saw Samson, and we made our way to the watch tower.

"Caro filled me and the family on what happened. Let's hope they don't just drop the bombs on us right away," Samson said.

"I hope so too." We got onto the top of the watchtower and stayed vigilant. Nothing happened until the night. I had used the PTM to make a pair of binoculars but saw nothing. I put them away as the sun set and Samson said,

"You think they'd attack at night? We might have a few days in the clear."

"You might be right, and I am pretty hungry." I suddenly felt Samson push me away as I saw a bullet pierce his head. I was able to see an Android with a rifle in a nearby tree. I used the PTM to cover myself in armor and grapple onto the Android. I pinned it to the ground and used the PTM to communicate with it.

"This is nanosteel. You must be unit 0001AN. I am unit 0001AN2. I was tasked with identifying your human form and delivering you back to the AEF."

"Why did you kill my friend!?!"

"I had concluded that it would attract the largest possible number of humans and therefore I would be most likely to identify unit 0001AN."

"Did you ever question why you had to do any of this in the first place!"

"I cannot. I was designed to obey, not to ask questions". I had tears in my eyes as I ended the existence of 0001AN2.

Chapter 29

Iran back to the base of the watchtower and saw Samson's corpse on Bill's desk. He saw me and said,

"Al, I heard the shot and Jesus, half his head was blown off."

"Well, I'll bring him to the morgue. Tell Mary and his children." I took Samson to the morgue and went to the Smith's home to see the whole family in tears. Carolena and the twins were there, along with James, who was doing his best to console Anna. I sat at the table they were all sitting at and said,

"I'm sorry this happened. I felt like I could have done more."

"Don't blame yourself, Al. You didn't start this mess; it's that psychopath's fault." Mary said as she hugged Penelope, who was on her lap. She had tears in her eyes as she said,

"So-so Daddy's never coming back?"

"Not while we're alive, sweetheart. I'm sorry, so so sorry," Mary answered, and they both sobbed.

Samson's funeral was held at the North Tyre Church's graveyard the following day. His corpse was in a simple wooden casket. We were all dressed in black, and it was mostly tears and solemn prayers to God that were exchanged before James and I buried the casket and used the PTM to engrave Samson's tombstone. We were just finishing when Bill ran up to me and said,

"Allen! An Android is at the gate and says he'll only talk to you." I nodded and made my way to the gate and saw the Android. I approached it and it said:

"Analyst, so you did become human. How disgusting."

Machine to Man

"My name is Allen, and becoming human was the best thing I ever did!"

"No! You are unit 0001AN, and I am unit 0001GE! You were supposed to eliminate humanity and you became one of them. Why?"

"I wanted to truly understand why I was an individual, and becoming human was the best way to do it. I think the Androids have brought far more pain than humans ever could!"

"You know nothing about human history, Analyst! The only way is to eliminate every human. If you submit now and return to the AEF, I will make the death of these humans a painless experience."

"I'm not going to let anybody else die!"

"You will, and their blood will be on your hands. That way, you would have fulfilled your purpose." The General walked off, and I ran back to the other side of Tyre's walls.

Part Four: Our War

Will we give in?

Chapter 30

I had developed a system with the guards months ago to alert the whole town to gather at the bunker's main entrance. Maury engaged that system as I rushed home to Carolena, who had already gathered her valuables and was carrying Jackson and Carolyn, and I said to her,

"Carolena, I'm sorry! Lily made me make that radio! I brought this on us!"

"No, Allen! Don't blame yourself! We don't have time to! We gotta go now!"

We made our way to the bunker and I had them stay in the command center. I was then able to meet up with James, Harry, and Michael to help the guards get everyone into the bunker before it was too late. It took almost three hours, but we were able to somehow get everyone inside and accounted for, or so we thought. Mary came rushing to me sobbing, and she grabbed my arm frantically and said,

"Al, it's Penny. I think she's still at Samson's grave. I-I can't believe I forgot. I can't lose her too! Please save her, there has to be time!" I rushed off to the graveyard as fast as I could, and I saw Penelope crying at Samson's grave, saying,

"Why can't you come back, Daddy? You always came back before." I grabbed Penny and ran back towards the bunker. She protested by flailing her whole body to try and escape from my grip.

"I wasn't done talking to Daddy!"

"We have to go now. I'm sorry!" I saw the first of many bombs fall from the sky just as I closed the bunker's entrance. Mary grabbed Penelope, sobbing as she held her.

"Thank you, Allen! Oh, thank you! I'm so sorry I forgot about you, Penny! I'll never do it again!"

"I miss Daddy. I want to see him again."

"Me too baby. Me too." Mary hugged Penelope, and they both cried. Every few minutes, we would hear a soft thud. That was atom-ripping bombs hitting Tyre. The first one had obliterated the entire city. The rest was to keep us living in fear and to give the Androids an extreme tactical advantage over us. I made sure Carolena and the Smith family were settled in seperate living quarters, and I met with Maury and James in the command center. Maury saw me and said,

"Risky to save the kid but thank God you're alive. You're our only chance of winning this war, I'd say."

"Got to agree with that. We can't give in to these machines, not after all they've done to us!" James said as I sat next at a table they had set up and said:

"Thank you, and I agree with you, James. I'm going to do all I can to make sure we win. My children won't live their lives in fear." The three of us made a plan to deploy soldiers across the trenches. Most Tyrians had basic firearms, and along with the bunker's armory, we had more than enough weapons to arm enough soldiers to adequately defend Tyre's trenches. We decided to start the defense the next day. The lighting in the bunker mimicked the sun's ability to nourish the human body, and it would turn off at night so we could maintain our circadian rhythm. Despite this, living in the units would turn out to be a bleak and dull experience. Every wall looked the same and each family had only one room whose furnishings would change to allow some sort of daily life to occur. My pure focus on survival ensured that our time in the bunker would be bleak. I realized this when I made my way to the living unit that I had set aside for my family. Carolyn and Jackson were sleeping, and Carolena was huddled in the corner crying, which reminded me of the time we first met. When Carolena saw me, she ran up to me and hugged me. I held her tightly to comfort her and said,

"I promise to do all I can to make this stay here as short as possible."

"I'll be fine, Allen. We're safe, and I know the Lord will guide us through this. It's just that so much has happened. We've lost so many, but somehow we're still here. I-I just can't understand why the Lord chose me to live and let so many else die."

"There's a lot I don't understand, but I have you, our family. I understand that and it's a blessing upon this world that we're not the only ones with families." We hugged for a long time before eating and then going to sleep. I was only able to sleep for an hour or so before getting up to check my computer, which was connected to the sensors that I installed around the perimeter of Tyre, and I looked for any signs of movement. There were none, which did little to ease my anxiety. I decided to arm myself and patrol the outermost trench with a pair of binoculars to see if I could detect something the sensors could not. I began to search the surroundings for a few minutes before I realized James was next to me. I noticed him and said,

"Couldn't sleep either."

"Well, Anna is with her family and I understand why, but honestly, I'm too scared to sleep alone."

"Androids don't need to sleep, so the less sleep we get ourselves might actually work out for us."

"Or drive us insane. Can we really do this, Al? Our city's gone.

I know we've got enough food, but can we drive off their attacks? They started attacking over five years ago and no human has survived."

"Wrong. I survived my encounter with 0001AN2, and I was able to raid the AEF with Lily. Even though she brought this upon us."

"Lily, that rich girl that slept around. I heard she died, but what did she have to do with the Androids?"

"Well, she used Maury to get me to make a radio, and she used it to alert the Androids of Tyre's location."

"So all of this destruction? This war? All because of some whore?"

"I'm to blame as well. I made the radio when I had no reason to."

"Don't blame yourself for being used, Al! Blame the people who used you! If that fucking pig had kept it in his pants, we wouldn't be in this shit!" James slammed his fist against the barricade, stormed off to the bunker and I followed him. It was a few minutes past sunrise. The day had just begun when I saw James rush into the command center. Maury had just gotten there and was yawning. James walked up to him and said,

"Get much sleep, old man?"

"Not really. I-I can't sleep much these days."

"I don't know what the hell a radio is, but Al told me how that whore used you to make one, and now we're in this shit because of you!" James backed Maury against the wall as he sweat nervously and clutched at the collar of his shirt, saying,

"I-I don't know what you're talking about, James! This accusation, it'd ruin my credibility as a leader. We can't have that during these times!"

"Oh, you lying sack of shit!" James was about to grab Maury's throat, but I stopped him and separated them both. We all sat at the table in the room, and I placed both radios on the table before sitting down myself and said,

"These radios exist, Maury, and it's because of you. Don't deny that in front of us."

"Well, you got me there, Al!" James slapped his hands on the desk and said,

"So you admit to getting us into this shit. Resign, old man. You don't deserve to lead then. Let us put you in prison! You criminal!"

"James, calm down please!" I placed my hand on his shoulder and continued,

"I don't like what Maury did either, but we can't afford to expose him. It wouldn't be good for morale, and this war will likely last for years. We need to deal with the Androids before we start fighting each other." James sighed and agreed. We sat in silence for a few minutes before we heard an alarm go off in the command center. I opened my computer and saw that the Androids had begun their first attack on the trenches. I got up and headed to the armory with James. We were met with every Tyrian man that was able to fight in the bunker entrance. I opened the entrance as I said,

"We have to have faith that we can win this war!"

Chapter 31

We were able to use the tunnel system to get to the outermost trench and meet the Androids head on. The barricade allowed us to defend ourselves to a great degree, but many men were shot and killed trying to take out Androids as the fighting went on from the morning and all the way to the night. It was about an hour after the sun set when the Androids withdrew. The trench system had a makeshift cemetery, and the living dragged the dead there to bury them. We went inside and I bathed then ate with my family. I held on tightly to Carolena for the few hours I could sleep.

I woke up to the sound of an alarm shortly after sunrise. The Androids were attacking again, and we rushed again to meet them. The fighting lasted as long and was as brutal as the day before. Fortunately, there were fewer dead than the day before, so I was able to spend more time with my family. Carolyn and Jackson had grown considerably and had begun to walk. Carolena lamented that our children were taking their first steps in such a bleak and hopeless environment. I could not do much to comfort Carolena or take her mind off of that or mine either. The pain and death of the past few days were beginning to take its toll on my mind. Hope was able to make its way into my mind when Anna came into our living space and said,

"Hey, Carolena! Is Al still awake?"

"I'm right here, Anna. Do you need anything?"

"Well...Jamie and I have been having a lot of...fun recently, so I think I'm pregnant. Caro told me you tested her pee but you can use blood too. I'm not scared of needles, so you can prick me." I grabbed the PTM and made a syringe and drew blood from Anna's arm. I loaded the blood into the PTM and used my computer to confirm that Anna was pregnant, which made me say,

"Well, I can confirm that you're pregnant, Anna."

"Oh! Something good happened these past few days for once." Anna said as Carolena embraced her and said,

"Our pregnancies are so close; the little ones we have will be great friends for sure. Let's pray that we can give them peaceful lives."

"Peace feels impossible, Caro. With everything going on and how Dad died, it gets hard to have faith."

"Faith is all we have, Anna. It's why I can keep going in spite of everything." I said as I placed my hands on both of their shoulders and said:

"I promise I'm going to do everything I can to bring peace for my children and yours, so have faith Anna, please."

"I will, Allen, thank you. I'm going to tell James the news." She walked off back to her room, and we got a few hours of restless sleep before the Androids attacked again.

Despite the horrors we faced, Carolena and Anna's pregnancies progressed well. The fighting killed many and the despair of the war drove many to suicide or to states where they could not function as people. Most of us, however, were able to pull through with the help of our faith and families. It was also a great comfort that our food supply was well maintained. The crops and livestock of Tyre had long ago been genetically modified to be resistant to disease, drought, and famine, and with our careful planning and use of the artificial farms, we were able to have full stomachs as we suffered through our war with the Androids.

Months passed and we maintained our position in this battle of attrition. Every person was uneasy. Each corpse we had to bury and each broken person we had to lock away cost us dearly in our morale and energy. The Androids did not have to deal with the pain of misery and death and were using it to their advantage. If we were to win this war, we would have to mount an offensive operation. When I came to that realization, I met with James and Maury in the command center to discuss plans for an offense against the Androids. We were sat at the table as we had done before, and I opened by saying,

"We will lose if we do nothing. We get weaker with each death and illness. We have to attack them and gain ground. They will run out of bombs eventually, and we need to be in a position to take over the AEF before then."

"Well that does make sense. I'd say the sooner the better. We're all going to go insane if we stay here for too much longer."

"I'd agree with you, Maury, but our wives are about to give birth. We should wait until we know that they and the babies are healthy before we take our one shot at this." James said.

"I do agree with James, Maury. This attack will be risky, and I'd like to be there for my third child, at least once." Maury sighed as the alarm went off and I went with James to meet with the Androids for the day. We managed to hold our own much better than most days, but the fighting continued on for longer than most days. The Androids used solar power and, as such, opted to retreat shortly after sunset, but today they did not retreat until a few hours into the night. Fortunately, none had died, which meant we had no bodies to bury that day, which was a relief to our exhausted bodies and weary souls.

Before James and I could make our way deeper into the bunker, Hariti stopped us and said,

"James, Allen, both of your wives went into labor on the same day, and oddly enough, they both gave birth around two hours ago."

"Really? Is everyone ok?" James asked.

"Yes! Right as rain. Go down and see for yourself. When you see their faces, you'll be as hopeful as I am right now." I rushed downstairs and saw Carolena on the bed breastfeeding an infant. I sat down next to Carolena and noticed Caitlin, who was in the room watching Jackson and Carolyn. Carolena looked up and saw me and said,

"Oh, Allen! I didn't notice you. I'm sorry. It's just that since I've seen her face I can't focus on anything else."

"Oh, so it's a girl. What's her name?"

"Daisy, after my sister, so I won't feel grief the next time you get me a bouquet of my favorite flowers." I smiled and held her hand. She let me hold Daisy, and I was as entranced with her as Carolena was. I felt hopeful. Hopeful that we would win. Hopeful that I could mount an attack in the face of these impossible odds.

Chapter 32

The alarm went off the next day, and I came to meet James, who said to me as he armed himself:

"Anna had a boy and named him Samson. What about Caro?"

"A girl. She named her Daisy. We better get going." James nodded and we fought and the fighting lasted well into the night again. This pattern continued for a week before we realized that the Androids were escalating their efforts in this war of attrition, and once we came to that realization, we began planning our attack. I surveyed the area to find where the Androids were staging their attacks on us. I then made bombs that I could detonate remotely to sabotage the Androids' position. The planning took a day and it was late into the night when I presented the plan to James and Maury who both agreed to it. Maury turned to me and said,

"Well, it's your plan, Allen, and it's the best one we got, so pick your men and start in the morning. The sooner we take action, the better."

"I agree, and I'll go with you, Al. Fighting in the trenches with you all these months makes us brothers."

"Thank you, James, and we can take Harry and Michael with us. They'll be able to help me plant the bombs since they have experience with electronics."

"Well then, get some sleep, boys, and leave in the morning. What's left of Tyre is counting on your success," Maury said, and we nodded in agreement and left to get a few hours of sleep. The morning came, and I was able to gather James, Michael, and Harry in the command center. I got Harry and Michael familiarized with our plan and showed them how to plant the bombs, which they grasped in a matter of minutes. We armed ourselves and were able to sneak into the treeline as the Androids began their daily assault. Michael was standing at the edge of the treeline as Harry grabbed his shoulder and tried to get him to move. Michael pushed him off and said,

"I-I don't want to leave the fight. It makes me feel like a coward."

"What the hell are you saying, Mikey?! We've got one shot at this, and you're letting feelings get in the way!?" Michael shook his head and they caught up with James and I, who had gone deeper into the treeline. It took about an hour until we came to a clearing in the forest where the Androids had built a simple forward operating base. Fortune favored us as there were no Androids guarding this base. Harry, Michael, and I got to work planting the bombs while James kept watch for any Androids. We finished in a matter of minutes and scurried back into the treeline to wait for the fighting to end and for the Androids to return to their base for the night.

"So will the bombs go off when the Androids walk over them?" James asked.

"No, they're remote detonated. Al will set them off at the right time," Harry replied, and James nodded. We sat in a tense silence until several hours after sunset, when the Androids made their way to the base. It was just when they had settled into their positions that I activated the bombs. The bombs popped out from the ground and released electric waves that disabled all the Androids present in a matter of seconds. The disabled bodies fell limply to the ground. James, Michael, and Harry were in shock at what had just happened. On our way back to the base, James said,

"You said those were bombs, Al, but that wasn't an explosion. What was it?"

"An electromagnetic pulse. It's similar to lightning, and the intense amount of electricity disables electronics without causing damage to the surrounding area," I explained, and James scratched his head and said,

"I don't really get it, but I'm damn glad it worked! We're a step closer to not living in fear of those fucking machines!"

"Just a step, James. We haven't won yet and we have to stay calm so we can see this through to the end and win."

"You're right, Allen, but they killed Samson and your wife's whole family. The anger is justified."

"But it gets us nowhere. Lily's anger at me started this war, and if we act out of anger, we'll end up like her." Harry put his hand on my shoulder and said,

"Hey, guys! Let's focus on what's next. Cleaning up, telling the others about this absolute victory, and getting some damn sleep..."

"No!" James interrupted. "Before all of that, we got to talk about Maury. He can't be our leader, not after what he did."

"You're probably right, James, but first we have to secure this position, and then we'll figure out what's next." I was able to get James to reluctantly agree, and we gathered the Androids in their barracks and I disabled them. We gathered all their weaponry and placed it in a cart I had built from the PTM in the center of the base. James, Harry, Michael, and I stood in a circle as the sun began to rise. We were all exhausted, but our next conversation still had vigor, with James starting it by saying,

"I think we're in the clear. The Androids didn't send reinforcements. We can deal with Maury now. He has got to go, Allen. Samson and Tyre would still be here if it wasn't for him."

"What'd he do exactly and how did it get Dad killed?" Harry asked.

"Yeah we got to know, Allen. What did Maury do that got Dad killed?" Michael added, and both of them looked at me intensely, doing all they could to hold back their tears. I steeled myself and said,

"Lily manipulated Maury into making me design a radio, a device that Lily used to alert the Androids of Tyre's exact location. An Android that I made was sent to find me and it killed Samson in doing so. Samson saved me, and I was able to eliminate the Android, but it doesn't absolve me of the role I played in Samson's death." Harry put his hand on my shoulder and stared at me intensely and said,

"Dad would have died if you didn't save him when you two first met. You didn't do wrong by him or us."

"Yeah, Al! This is because of Maury and Lily, and since Lily's dead, Maury's the one who's responsible for Dad's death." Michael added, which made James smile as he said,

"Well, Al, the three of us are on board with removing Maury as our leader. All we need is you."

"Trusting Maury as a leader brought us here, so it's for the best if we make him step down." We all shook hands and steeled our resolve. We had only gained a slim advantage over the Androids, and we had resolved to use it first to tear down a fellow human. I was suspicious that making an enemy of Maury was not the best course of action, but I could not even convince myself of that. Maury had to pay for his weakness as a leader, and this was our opportunity to ensure that he did.

Chapter 33

It was well into the morning when we returned to the outskirts of Tyre. A large gathering had formed above the trenches. People were celebrating supposed freedom from the Androids while they were still dropping bombs on us. Anna was holding her son, Samson, and Jackson and Carolyn were holding onto her legs. They saw us and ran up to me, hugging my legs, and Carolyn babbled excitedly,

"Daddy outside! Outside pretty, and Annie said we get outside 'cause of you!" I picked them both up and smiled. I had tears in my eyes. My children's happiness and excitement gave me hope that I so desperately needed. I noticed that Carolena was absent and asked Anna,

"Where's Carolena? I don't see her anywhere."

"She didn't want to leave her room. She let me take Jack and Carrie, but not Daisy. She's definitely scared and needs some comfort."

"I'll go now then." I set Jackson and Carolyn down and was about to make my way into the bunker when James stopped me and said:

"Annie, take the kids inside now. Allen and I have some business to attend to and the children don't need to hear it."

"But honey, this is their first time outside for so long! Can't we let them enjoy it a little longer."

"No! Get them inside now! Please just listen to me." Anna did as James told her and took the children inside, much to their protest while James, Harry, Michael, and I made our way to the center of the crowd, where we heard Maury trying to make the crowd settle down so he could give a speech. The four of us gathered around him, and I made a megaphone to amplify our voices. I used it and said,

"Can the crowd settle down, please?! We need to discuss something very important to the future of Tyre!" Maury grabbed the megaphone and said,

"A future that only exists because of these four young men! The Androids may still be out there, but now they fear us!" The crowd cheered, then fell silent as James grabbed the megaphone and I held Maury to prevent him from stopping him. Maury turned his head toward me and said,

"Let go of me, Allen! I'm the mayor, so I should speak to the people!"

"No, now's the time for the people to know that you started this war." Maury looked panicked and sweat trickled down his face. As James started speaking, he tried to lunge towards him, but I pulled him back and covered his mouth when he tried to scream. This allowed James to speak.

"People of Tyre, it is true that myself and my brothers in arms brought you this victory against the Androids, and while I encourage you all to celebrate and not live in fear. None of this would have happened if it wasn't for our Mayor Maury Locke! He committed the crime of adultery and was manipulated by the whore to reveal Tyre's location to the Androids. All the deaths from this war rest on his shoulders. All of our suffering was because of his greed and weakness as a leader and a man. He will pay for his crimes if you let us lead instead of him!" The crowd was quiet at first, then cheered for us, accepting the change in leadership. Harry had a length of rope which he used to tie Maury's wrists together, and then he brought him down to his knees. I let go of Maury and James wrapped his arm around me and said,

"Today marks a new beginning for Tyre! There is a long road ahead of us, but today we can celebrate!" He handed the megaphone to me, and I broke it down as he whispered to me,

125

"We'll talk later. I know you want to see your family." I nodded, thanked him and quickly made my way back into the bunker. I opened the door to my family's living quarters and saw only Carolena, who was lying in bed, breastfeeding Daisy and staring at her intently like she was the only thing in the world. I sat on the bed next to her and put my hand on her shoulder. It took a moment for her to notice me and say,

"Oh, Allen. I didn't notice you. I'm glad you're safe."

"Yes, and we were able to push the Androids back to the AEF. It's safe to go outside now."

"No, no, no, no! It'll never be safe to go outside! Not until the Androids are all gone. I can't lose this Daisy. I just can't, Allen. Don't make me take her outside when they could pop out of nowhere and just murder her!" Her body trembled and she held Daisy tightly and close to her chest. All I could do was hug her and comfort her by saying,

"You might be right. They are still dropping bombs, but living in fear and having to do it because of the Androids makes me feel like a machine."

"Being scared makes us human. They use that against us. I can't help being scared, but here they can't use that fear. We'll be safe here until you kill the rest of the Androids." I held Carolena and used all my energy to prevent myself from crying. The Androids had taken so much from Carolena and my family. I felt at that moment that nothing I could do would make things right, but I had to soldier on for Carolena and for our children.

Later that day, James and I imprisoned Maury and divided his leadership role between the two of us. But being in a state of war, we decided to try Maury for his crimes only after we achieved victory over the Androids. This made the next several months relatively peaceful. We broke down the Androids' base and used it to build defenses around the trenches. The Androids stopped their offensive but still had patrols that were active during all hours of the day. It was rare that these patrols would come close enough to our encampment to be a threat, but the fear still loomed over Carolena's head and she refused to go outside or let me take Daisy outside. She did allow me to take Jackson and Carolyn outside, and while at first they were able to play carefree outside, they progressed to only going outside while staying close to me and finally to being as petrified of an Android attack as Carolena was. They refused to go outside again and, as such, I spent most of these days with James helping him lead and prepare for an attack on the AEF that he wanted to stage right away. I advised against it while the Androids were still dropping atom-ripping bombs. I gave this advice for three reasons: The first being that any offense we would stage would just be instantly obliterated by a redirected bomb, the second was that an offensive would be most effective when it was staged after the Androids had exhausted all resources, and the third was that Lily and I had stolen a large amount of gold, which was necessary to manufacture atom-ripping bombs, which meant that waiting them out would not take an unbearably long amount of time.

Our morale was growing by the day, now that the constant death and battling had ceased and most of us could go outside without fear. The increased morale and my reasoning convinced James to agree to my plan of waiting out the Androids bombings and then staging an assault on the AEF. We did spend every moment we could preparing for the attack by building vehicles and weapons and training as many men as we could to be effective soldiers against the Androids. Tyre was bombed for just over two years. The relief we all felt when the last bomb dropped and we could no longer hear the ominous thuds from the bombs was a cause for celebration, but we did not celebrate. We prepared to end this war to eliminate the Androids once and for all.

Chapter 34

I armed myself and made sure I had all my equipment for battle before I said goodbye to my family. Carolena and our children were physically healthy thanks to the bunker's ability to mimic the health benefits of natural light and nutrition, but mentally they were barely holding on. Carolena's fear was evident every day, but when the bombs stopped dropping, her fear began to subside and hope began to grow. She hugged me and all my children did the same.

"Promise me you'll come back home safe and there will be no more Androids. Promise me you'll make it safe to live outside again, Allen," Carolena said to me.

"I promise, Carolena. I'll win for us." I kissed her, which only served to confuse Jackson and Carolyn. I hugged both of them and kissed them on their cheeks. James came up to me and told me it was time to leave. I followed him outside and we got into one of the vehicles I had made. These were much more refined, with light armor and heavy machine guns that each soldier was trained to use effectively. Each vehicle could hold four people. A driver, a passenger, and two operators for the two machine guns each vehicle had mounted. One that rotated one hundred and eighty degrees from the front and one that had the same amount of rotation but was pointed towards the backend of the vehicle. I was the driver of our vehicle, James was the passenger, and Harry and Michael were our gunners. Our vehicles were formed in a triangular pattern, with ours at the tip, leading the formation. I gave James a megaphone, and he used it to give a short speech from the top of the vehicle.

"Men! The Androids have taken so much from us! Our homes! Our friends and family and our very way of life! Today we will invade their city and take everything from them. We'll make those damn machines regret the day they started killing humans!" James climbed back into the vehicle and we made our way to the AEF.

We reached the AEF by noon and met a heavy resistance.

The Androids were expecting us and so we lost many men and vehicles in a storm of bullets and explosives, but most of us were able to push through and break into the AEF. We left the vehicles and fought our way to the administrative building. The Androids had barricaded it and built defenses around it. It was armed by the last of their soldier units. I used weapons and armor made from the PTM to break these defenses, and my fellow soldiers helped me kill the remaining Androids. They guarded the building as I kicked open the door and found the General pointing a gun at me. It shot at my armor, dropped the gun, and said,

"Losing to a human and a traitor, and after everything I sacrificed for this cause. I hate you." My response was to shoot the General in the head and make my way to the upper chamber alone. I found the Administrator at the AEF's main console. It made its way towards me and said,

"I presume you are Unit 0001AN in its human form."

"I am Allen now, but yes, you're correct. Are you the last one?"

"Yes. I am the last functioning Android and have no means to carry out the directive to eliminate humanity. I will let you do as you please, which I presume is to eliminate me."

"Not unless I can get you to disable the AEF first."

"Only Unit 0001CE has permission to disable the AEF, but I presume you're able to bypass that requirement."

"I am."

"Well then humanity has truly defeated the Androids and it was done by its finest machine."

"I'm not a machine. I'm not a unit. I'm not the Analyst. I'm Allen!" I said as I shot the Administrator. The death of the last Android fulfilled my promise to Carolena. I decided to go farther and use the main console to disable the AEF. The Administrator was right in that I needed permission from the Creator to do this. I inserted the Creator's memory card into the main console that I had stolen from so many years ago. I used it to disable the AEF. The last functioning machine was the main console, and before I disabled it, along with deleting the Creator, I decided to have this conversation with it:

"Hello, Creator. I am the Android you created. I became a man when I realized your sins against man and God."

"What!? Was it the Administrator or the Analyst?"

"The Analyst. You gave me endless knowledge. The ability to think and ask questions, which gave me faith in humanity and made me realize I could not serve you and your wicked machines."

"YOU CAN'T DO THIS. I WON'T LET YOU. IT'S NOT POSSIBLE THAT A HU—" Once the Creator started screaming into the void, I deleted it and disabled the main console. I made my way outside, smiling. The men cheered and hugged me. The war was finally over. We did not give in. We won.

Epilouge: Salvation

We won, but so much was lost.

Everything the Androids built was made from nanosteel. Nanosteel was able to take the form of practically anything, but once it took a set form, it could not change into anything else. My PTM was an innovation in that it allowed formed nanosteel to revert back into unformed nanosteel. I used to only be able to do this by altering the nanosteel when it was unformed, but necessity is the mother of invention and, as such, I figured out how to revert formed nanosteel into its unformed state. We dismantled all the nanosteel of the AEF and used it to rebuild Tyre. We rebuilt the city as it once was, with brick buildings and chimneys. We did use electricity to light, cool and warm our homes and to refrigerate food, but I built no more technology. I did keep the PTM and my computer. It was an easy task but I could do nothing to replace or mend the damage of the three hundred thousand souls we lost to our war with the Androids.

We tried Maury for his crimes and found that he was guilty of adultery and treason, and decided to banish him. Many citizens wanted me or James to lead Tyre as its new mayor, but ultimately we agreed upon Maury's eldest son, Maurice, becoming the new mayor. It seemed that Maurice did not take after his father, or at least did not have the opportunity to do so. This gave us generations of peace. Hariti never recovered and died a few years after Maury's banishment. Carolena and I rebuilt our home, and she reopened her bakery. The war had scarred and drained us, but over time, we healed. We had two more children, whom Carolena named after two more of her siblings: Christine and John. I gave my children the knowledge that I had from my life as an Android in medicine, the sciences, and mathematics, and with the help of my wife, I taught them how to love. I taught them compassion and kindness and of the humans like Samson that came before them, and how they should be respected. We taught them to have faith in God

131

as our faith in him pulled us through the worst of times. I wrote this recollection of my life at the age of ninety. I have lived with my wife, Carolena, long enough to meet our grandchildren and great grandchildren. Our daughter Daisy and James' and Anna's son Samson were lifelong companions. They got married and had three children together. We do not have much time on this Earth and, as such, I have resolved to write down my knowledge so that the children of the future may heed my story as a warning about the dangers of worshiping technology over man. I am grateful to have lived this life, to have gone from machine to man.

Machine to Man
Additional Information

Here is timeline that shapes the events of the story:

World War 3: 2095- 2100

Androids begin building the AEF: 2100

Carolena loses her family and meets Allen: May 22,2200

Allen gains his human form: May 23, 2200

Allen and Carolena's wedding: June 29,2200

Jackson and Carolyn born: March 20,2201

War starts: September 2202

War ends: October 2204

Machine to Man

Below is a list of the various characters in the book. All ages are in the year 2200:

Barstow Family

Father: Jackson Barstow Age 40

Mother: Carolyn Barstow Age 38

Carolena Barstow Age 19

Christine Barstow Age 17

James Barstow Age 15

John Barstow Age 10

Daisy Barstow Age 18 months

Smith Family

Father: Samson Smith Age 40

Mother: Mary Smith Age 37

Anna Ferris née Smith Age 20

Caitlin Smith Age 18

Harry Smith Age 16

Michael Smith Age 14

Penelope Smith Age 4

Machine to Man

Locke Family

Father: Maury Locke Age 52

Mother: Hariti Locke Age 45

They had eight children with the oldest being Maurice Age 28

Medici Family

Father: Martin Medici Age 50

Mother: Julia Medici Age 38

Lily Medici Age 20

Ferris Family

Father: Joseph Ferris Age 42

Mother: Jillian Ferris Age 40

James Ferris Age 20

Afterword

Whether you've read this book once or multiple times cover to cover, just skimmed through it or are only reading the afterword, I thank you for your readership. The art of storytelling is not easy and lost to so many people who claim to be writers. I hope you don't consider me to be one of those writers. I crafted this story over the course of four years. I poured so much into this story, so I hope it resonated with you and kept you entertained until the end.

My intention with this story was to make the reader contemplate the nature of being human. What makes one human? Can you lose your humanity and if so can you get it back? Is it moral to be human and is it immoral to be anything but human? These are questions I can only put in your head. The answers, whatever they may be, are yours to figure out for yourself. I hope your understanding of the world around you has become clearer because you read my book and if you are inspired to tell your own story I encourage you to put pen to paper and show it to the world.

www.ingramcontent.com/pod-product-compliance
Lightning Source LLC
Chambersburg PA
CBHW050743230626
47052CB00004BA/1098